JOSEPH FALLEN
(Estate Series – Book 0.5)

By M.S. Willis

OTHER BOOKS BY M.S. WILLIS

Control Series

Book One – Control

Book Two – Conflict

Book Three – Conquer

Estate Series

Book One – Madeleine Abducted

Coming in 2014

Because of Ellison

Hope Restrained (Estate Series #2)

Captured (Control #4)

Changed (Control #5)

Table of Contents

Prologue

There are stories that are too painful to tell. Although, better left buried within the deep recesses of the minds of those who lived them, those stories never truly leave a person. But they must be told, because, even in their silence, they can affect and shape the future of others.

This is one of those stories...

You may think you know what happened, the supposed knowledge acting as a warm and gratifying blanket that protects you from the darkness; A seemingly innocuous barrier between a person and the truth.

You know how this ends and you must be acutely aware that there is no anticipation of an uplifting and inspired ending. But what you don't know is why...

He was a good man. One who envisioned the life of a successful businessman; a wife, a child and a sprawling mansion so large, most could not help but envy the lifestyle achieved by such a handsome, charismatic and intelligent person. He was a genius. He deserved his youthful accomplishments. But like every sorrowful tale, that achievement became a poison; one that allowed darkness to seep inside --- to imbed itself so far within his soul that reality twisted and insanity followed.

His name was Joseph Carmichael and when he started The Estate, he not only created Hell...

He ruled it.

Chapter One

"Joseph, you shouldn't have."

Laughing seductively, Arianna Carmichael lifted the golden curtain of her hair from around her shoulders while her adoring husband, Joseph, locked the clasp of a diamond necklace across the perfection of her sun-kissed skin. It was their honeymoon. Much like when they'd dated, Joseph lavished what he could on the woman who lifted his spirits. She was a balm; a soul who could soothe the machinations of his brilliant mind, and a spirit that infused him with so much beauty and light, he could barely function without having her in his life. When it came to Arianna, there was no posturing, no political manifesto by which he had to operate; it was simply love - pure, honest, and absolute.

With blue eyes that resembled dancing flames, she peered up at him through the mirror of the dark wood dressing table. Glancing down at her reflection, he realized they were both lost to their bond, one that had been established only a few years prior, but one that had driven Joseph to achievements not known by most men his age. Although only twenty-three, Joseph had excelled in his education, had graduated early and was in line to become a top-seated executive in the large corporation where he'd accepted his first job.

It was while attending a holiday gala that he'd first seen Arianna. She was the epitome of elegance when she walked into the room. She attracted the attention of each man in attendance when the light bounced off the champagne colored fabric of her gown. Gracefully, she traveled the room, her movement so fluid it appeared that she floated on air. He wanted her the moment he saw her and when their eyes met across the crowded space, the people in the room disappeared from around them. Their love was instantaneous, their relationship was destined, and their partnership was spoken about as an ideal to which every couple should strive.

Letting the necklace fall across her shoulders, he clasped her hand and swept her up from her chair, leading her immediately through a suggestive and provocative dance across the expansive bridal suite. Music drowned the atmosphere and the light swish of her wedding gown could also be heard from their movement. A goddess dressed in white, Joseph admired how beautiful she looked in the dress, but also anticipated the moment when he'd remove it. He'd not slept with her before they were married, could not bear to tarnish the purity of a woman he'd never felt he'd deserved. But now, she was his wife, and his body molded to her while they danced, every nerve along his skin burning with his need to feel her wrapped around him and the slide of her sweat-soaked skin against his. His face brushed across her hair as they spun, and his heart swelled when her delicate scent wrapped around him like a soft caress or a tender touch.

In a wistful tone, he teased, "Have I ever mentioned how much of a gift you are? You may have made a mistake today, *Mrs. Carmichael*, by marrying a man not worthy of your perfection."

The responsive laughter was a delight to his ears. She smiled up at him with an expression that revealed the truth of her exhilaration in that moment. Her head fell back as he dipped her low to the ground; sweeping its way across the burgundy carpet before being pulled back to her body when she was once again lifted and held against his chest. "I don't know about that. There are rumors that I am not worthy of you. Apparently, I've failed to pay my dues to your society, not having come from old money and not having the education granted to the women whose fathers can afford it."

He brought her arm above her head as he spun her softly along the floor, and when her back was to his, he pulled her to him so that he could rest his mouth softly against the rim of her delicate ear. "Jealous bitches...all of them. They wouldn't last one day with me with their inane babble and superficial bullshit. But, if you want, I could see to it that we never hear from them again..." His mouth twisted up slightly at his mischievous suggestion. "...Maybe I could pay someone to intimidate them into silence." His brows bounced, making Arianna laugh loudly.

Turning towards him, she slapped her hand against his shoulder, and said, "You wouldn't do that, Joseph. You are far too intelligent to do anything stupid because of the opinions of petty and pathetic women. If they were in any way happy with their own lives, they wouldn't waste their time trashing mine."

He twirled her again then held her apart from him so that he could look deep into the blue depths of her eyes. With a wicked grin, he responded, "You're absolutely right. Intimidation would be stupid. Death from an unfortunate *accident* will be a more permanent approach."

Arianna laughed again, her hair flowing behind her while she was danced through the room. The music slowed, faded off into silence, and Joseph chose that quiet moment to take her mouth with his. What started as a gentle and heartfelt kiss quickly grew in its intensity; their fingers entangled into each other's hair as the two lovers became desperate to converge with the person they desired.

Pulling away from his bride, Joseph's eyes traveled down over her skin, down further along the lace bodice of her gown and the white satin that danced like deliquescent pearl along her hips and legs. She was stunning and his heart beat furiously at the sight of her while he attempted in vain to shake the prickling anger in his mind towards the women he knew spoke poorly of his wife.

Ferocity and tenacious anger flooded his eyes when he looked into her face once more. "Those women, I can't stand what they say about you. I'll let it go for tonight, but I won't allow them to continue their attack once the honeymoon is over. I don't care what type of money, society, or esteemed family they come from; you are now my wife, and as such, you are a part of me."

His words startled Arianna in their sincerity. Quietly, she responded, "I don't need your protection, Joseph. I'm perfectly capable of ignoring their rumors - as long as I know the truth behind their lies, than what they say doesn't matter."

After brushing away the hair that had fallen in her face when they'd danced, he said, "Let's forget about them. That is not what this night is about." Forcing a smile on his face, he watched as Arianna beamed back in response.

His hands reached behind her to find the tiny white buttons that trailed along the center of her gown. Frustrated with the amount of buttons he'd encountered, Joseph dramatically rolled his eyes as he openly lamented how long it would take to remove the gown from her body. "You would think that the designer of this particular dress would have a better understanding of how quickly it is meant to be removed. How many buttons are there exactly?"

A giggle escaped her rouge stained lips, and Arianna stepped back, nearly tripping over the train of the gown. "Here – allow me. Buttons such as these are meant for a far more nimble finger."

Watching his bride reach behind her back, a soft growl emanated from his chest as the bodice of her gown gave way. With each slight motion to her arm, the dressed peeled down, no longer acting as a second skin to her incredible form, but becoming nothing more than the clothing used to attract the attention of her intended betrothed. As the dress descended to the ground, it puddled at her feet creating a barrier she had to step over to be completely freed of the fabric.

His breath caught, his eyes left unblinking as a shudder trembled a path along his skin, through his muscles and into his bones. He'd known she was beautiful, but to see her standing in nothing more than the corset bra and delicate silk panties she'd worn under her dress, it caused his body to quake in anticipation and to marvel at her transformation from splendid innocence into mesmerizing temptation.

Stepping forward, Joseph brushed the back of his hand along her face, down along her jaw, past her shoulder, to finally rest just above the swell of her breasts and over her rapidly beating heart. The steel grey of his eyes remained locked to the infinite blue of hers; he noticed how her chest heaved and how her skin prickled in expectation of what was to come.

Refusing to look away from the eyes of the woman that had bewitched him years before and who had held him in wonderment since the day they'd first met, he said, "When I take you tonight, you will finally and completely become mine. I'll never fail you, I'll always protect you and I will give you the life that only a woman of your caliber deserves. Thank you, Arianna, for giving me a reason to live, a reason to breathe, and a reason to succeed. If it is you that I am allowed to care for, I can achieve anything, even if it breaks me apart to do so."

The low light of the room sparkled brilliantly off the diamond ring on her finger when she reached up to place her hand over his. Rapidly, her blood surged through her veins and they both felt the beat of her heart against their joined hands. Her eyelids fluttered; her body overtaken by the anticipation of his touch mixed with the remnants of the alcohol they'd drank at the wedding just hours before.

He watched the full pout of her lips curve when she spoke, the moisture glistening in the light, making him imagine what those lips would feel like along his heated skin. "We'll take care of each other, Joseph. Not one above the other, not one weak and one strong – but beside each other. My love for you knows no bounds and I will give to you everything that I have and accept from you everything that you are willing to give."

Their words closely resembled the vows they'd just spoken at the alter of the cathedral church where'd they'd been married. Joseph reached his arm around her waist, pulling her against him as he allowed his fingers to slowly travel down her back and over the fine silk of her panties. When her body trembled beneath his hold, his breath was wrenched from his lungs. His head moved forward, his lips taking hers, as his body moved to possess her fully.

Lifting her into his arms, he swiveled towards the large bed that sat unrumpled in the center of the room. Placing her on the bed, he pulled her into a sitting position and reached around in another attempt at freeing her from her clothes. When his large fingers slipped easily over the small clasps of her bra, she laughed again and shook her head in amusement. Their eyes met, hers crinkled at the sides from her mirth and his, wide-opened in astonishment at the depth of his feelings towards the woman before him. Her legs slipped open where they hung over the edge of the mattress, he pressed closer between them, watching while she removed the lacy boned garment from her breasts.

When she'd been freed of all but the small triangle of silk stretched taut between her thighs, his pants tightened while his eyes took in the smooth expanse of her naturally tan skin. Stunned momentarily, he sat frozen before her, a man sitting in reverence of a woman unlike any other he'd known.

"You are the most beautiful sight I've ever seen – and to think that you are mine, always..."

"...And forever." She smiled shyly.

Eyes the color of polished steel widened when she completed his statement. "Yes, Arianna...forever."

Taking her mouth with his, he licked along the crease of her lips demanding entry as his hands traveled to his shirt to slowly and deftly undo the buttons. Never allowing his lips to leave hers, he slowly peeled off the shirt, dropping it to the floor beside him. Pushing himself up from his crouched position, his hands came to her shoulders and he moved her back to the center of the bed and finally released her kiss so that he could remove his pants. He noticed how her eyes watched as he undid the button and lowered the zipper, eventually freeing himself of the offensive material that was the only thing keeping him from burying himself in her at that moment. Her breath caught when he was finally completely bared to her and he slid what remained of her undergarments from her body.

Lying over his bride, Joseph shimmied himself between her legs, positioning himself to finally and fully take her as his. "I don't want this to hurt you, tell me if it is too much."

She smiled up at him, however her nervousness could be seen as a sheen in her beautiful blue eyes. "Will you use protection? I could get pregnant..."

Placing a single finger over her mouth, Joseph silenced her. "You are my wife. If we conceive a child tonight, than it is a gift of our marriage, a blessing bestowed on us on the night we were married. We are a family now, and I do not fear building upon it."

Arianna settled beneath Joseph and he brought his mouth to hers once more. His hands traveled along the prickled skin of her stomach and torso, the rush of blood through her veins pounding against his hand as he felt her skin heat and flush at his touch. His large hand came up to cup the weight of her breast and a sigh escaped her perfectly pouted lips, now swollen from the force of his kiss. His fingers pinched the tip of her breast into a taut peak just as he kissed his way down her skin, finally taking the nipple of her breast between his lips and allowing his tongue to lave across the tip. She pressed her body up into his face, begging for more while he allowed his other hand to reach down towards the apex of her thighs. Finding that her skin had already slickened with desire he worked her body into frenzied need, until her breath came in erratic spurts and her heart could be heard pounding against the walls of her chest.

When she'd come close to orgasm, he slowed down the actions of his hands and mouth and looked up into her hooded gaze. "I believe I'll be taking you now, Mrs. Carmichael."

Her mouth formed a fevered grin and her eyes rolled back as he began to push himself inside her in one slow, yet deft maneuver. The wet heat of her body molded over him like a glove, and once buried to the hilt, he stopped, checking her face for any sign of discomfort before moving within her, building from an excruciatingly slow rhythm to one that would send them both over the edge into ecstasy.

The muscles of her core gripped at him hungrily and her head fell back against the pillows. When her mouth opened to scream out his name, he released himself inside her, claiming her as his. He fell against her, their sweat slickened skin creating a luscious and lustful sensation across their bodies. Their hearts pounded in unison and Joseph looked down at his sated bride and almost wept at the beauty that lay beneath him.

They made love several times that night, lost in the splendor and astonishment of their lust. While falling asleep in the early hours of morning, Joseph's eyes closed against the tendrils of light that peeked around the curtains of the room, and he held Arianna to his chest, the decision overwhelming his mind that she would be his forever and he would build a kingdom worthy of her alone.

Chapter Two

"Congratulations, Joseph. For someone of your age, your accomplishments within the company are a first. Usually, a man needs to be greying and wrinkled before finding a top seat within the executive offices. Yet, here you are, not only running this show, but taking it over from the owners. I wish I'd had your enthusiasm and skill as a younger man. It would have saved me many years chained to my desk for those bastards."

Joseph sat back in the soft cushion of his chair, the leather groaning against his weight as he propped his feet up on the mahogany expanse of the large wooden desk. Behind him, a panoramic view of the city was portrayed through the picture windows that encased the office that he'd recently acquired.

It had been a year since he'd married Arianna and his love for his wife had pushed him up the corporate ladder due to his determination to provide her with the lifestyle that would surpass the heiresses who'd spoken ill of her when they'd first been married. They'd not yet conceived a child, and, instead, used the time to worship each other in the late evening hours they had together.   Although his days were spent in grueling business meetings, his evenings were spent in her loving arms or resting on a sofa in their modest home as she played her piano for him alone. Her mastery of the instrument was extraordinary and he'd encouraged her to play publicly so that people would understand what true talent sounded like. However, she always declined, preferring the seclusion of their home to the fame that would come with unveiling her talent to the world. Although he enjoyed hearing her play classical pieces written years before by famous composers, it was the songs that she wrote for him that brought his heart unfettered joy.

Snapping his attention back to the man sitting across from him in his office, Joseph smiled, his hands folded across his lap as he eyed the sharp-dressed business associate from across the smooth surface of his desk.

"I intend to become a very wealthy man, Hamilton. Every dime I've made, I've returned to this company. My *enthusiasm* is nothing more than well thought out plotting. I knew the owners were close to retirement, and I bought out their shares as quickly as I could. In this business, it is skill and careful planning that will lead you to the top. Acquisitions and subsequent sales of struggling companies comes a close second to the finesse required to keep an operation such as this performing at its peak."

A single eyebrow rose above Hamilton's eye, revealing that the man believed himself more apt for the position taken quietly by Joseph within the company. Although Joseph had started his career with the best of intentions, he'd quickly learned that a touch of cutthroat maneuvering had been required to best his peers in their race to the top. His morality had been placed aside when he undertook buying failing companies with the promise of building them up, but instead, stripping them of their assets so that his company continued to profit off the sweat of those less intelligent in business. Morality had no place in his position, a lesson learned quickly as Joseph positioned himself for success.

Hamilton settled back into the wing-backed chair in which he sat. His jaw ticked furiously even though he attempted to disguise his jealousy and anger at having been bested by a man twenty years his junior. "I look forward to the ball this evening. I'm sure you must be nervous being the guest of honor at a gathering of such powerful men in the field."

Joseph knew Hamilton was attempting to shake him, but laughed to himself realizing that Hamilton's words only revealed the anxiety of the man who was so obviously aware of Joseph's superiority. He was nothing if not a good judge of character. He never listened to a man's words, but rather he watched his actions, his body language, anything that would unerringly reveal the true thoughts of the person he was observing. Running his hand through the silk of his ebony hair, Joseph relaxed against the leather seat, eventually returning his hand to the desk to idly play with a pen that sat on the surface of the wood.

Flippantly he responded to Hamilton's attempt at ruffling his feathers. "Actually, I've been looking forward to it. When rubbing elbows with men of such wealth, it is entirely possible that some of that money will be rubbed off on me. And we both know that the more money I have, the more powerful I will become."

A scowl lit Hamilton's face. Straightening his posture, he opened his mouth to speak again but was interrupted by a knock at the door.

"Come in." Joseph's baritone voice was brusque while giving permission to the unexpected visitor to enter. The bottom edge of the door brushed across the carpet and Arianna peaked her head around, her blue eyes seeking out the familiar grey of her husband's. When she spotted Hamilton sitting across from Joseph, she gasped and her hand reached to her mouth in surprise before her eyes shot back to Joseph.

"Oh, I'm so sorry. I didn't know you had…"

"Don't be silly. Come in." Standing immediately from his chair, Joseph stepped quickly through the room to greet his wife. She was dressed modestly in a knee length, A-line skirt with a buttoned blouse tucked at the waist and he couldn't help but marvel that, even in her casual clothing, she appeared like a jewel sparkling in the early morning sunlight that filtered in through the windows of his office.

Arianna's eyes wandered over her husband, her admiration of the way his suit fit over his muscular form apparent in the gleam in her eye. Even though they'd been married for a year, he still caught her hungry stares and secretive glances. He couldn't hold it against her though; because when she was in his presence, he was unapologetic in the way his eyes remained glued to her.

Without glancing back at his waiting colleague, Joseph said, "Hamilton, I'm afraid you will need to leave. Something important has just come up." He winked at Arianna, causing her to chuckle quietly.

Hamilton rose from his seat, pulling his jacket down from where it had gathered at his waist. "Of course. I'll see you both this evening, I'm sure." When Hamilton approached the doors, Joseph reached out for his wife's hand, pulling her towards him to give his associate enough room to exit. His other hand reached out to close the door as soon as Hamilton was fully outside.

He wasted no time in pressing his wife's small body up against the wall of his office, his hand moving quickly in its quest up her skirt. She laughed but was rapidly silenced when he settled his fingers against the apex of her thighs.

Lowering his head, he pressed his lips against her ear while circling the sensitive flesh between her legs. "What a pleasant surprise, Mrs. Carmichael. Please tell me you've come to give me good news."

A responsive moan escaped her glossed lips and Joseph bent lower to bite along the sensitive skin of her neck, pressing his hardened cock against her leg as he trapped her between his large body and the wall. She trembled against him and a smile escaped the corners of his sculpted mouth as her overtook her. He found both of her hands and pulled them above her head, pinning them to the wall above her head. When his lips continued their assault of the skin along her neck and jawline, he could feel her chest pounding against his from her lungs growing desperate for more air.

"Jo...Joseph – how can I talk when you're doing that?" Her voice was breathy and her body relaxed against the wall, her submission to her husband an instantaneous thing.

"Will you stop me?" His deep voice brushed across her skin like static electricity, heightening her desire as the vibration of the sound rattled along her nerve endings.

Peeking up at his ever-watchful face through the thickness of her lashes, she smiled sweetly. "Have I ever?"

Releasing her hands, Joseph reached down to grab his wife's legs pulling them up and around his waist. He was appreciative of the loose skirt, allowing him access to every part of her. Reaching back to bury his finger slowly, yet deeply, inside her, he continued talking to her, enjoying her raspy responses to his questions.

"Do you have news for me, beautiful? I know your appointment was this morning. I expected a phone call, but this will do as well." He continued working her toward an edge he'd seen her tumble over so many times before. He observed her lips moving, as if to speak, but no sound came forth except for her needful panting and tortured moans. When her eyes rolled back in her head, Joseph gave her the release she sought, his breath catching in his lungs to watch a sated expression fall over the face of an angel.

When she'd regained herself, Joseph smiled down at her. Grasping her body within his arms, he pulled her from the wall and carried over to the couch where he sat her down. Her head rested against his chest and their legs entangled where they hung over the side. Finally reaching a point where she could speak again, a saddened look came over her features when she looked up into his face.

"I'm not pregnant, Joseph. My, well, I'm late, but the tests came back negative."

His shoulders fell as the expectation in his body blew out on his released sigh. He wanted to give in to his own disappointment, but when he viewed the look on Arianna's face, he forced himself to step up to reassure her.

Holding her chin in his hand, he smiled down at her. "Then I guess we'll try again. Over and over, until it takes. Some of the best things on Earth are the things you must wait for. This only tells me that our child will be special...a gift given to us when we least expect it."

Grinning up at him, a single tear escaped her eye and Joseph reached over to wipe it from her face. "Don't cry my love, it will happen, and when it does, I'll scream out my triumph over the entire city. Every person will know that the love of my life is pregnant with my child. You'll be the most beautiful – and round – woman out there."

Her melodic laughter washed over him, and he continued teasing her to bring her back from her threatened despair. Finally, when all sadness had been vanquished from her eyes, he pulled her into his lap, resting his head against hers as he reminded her of their plans that evening.

"Are you looking forward to the ball tonight?"

Arianna nodded her head. "Yes. It's not often that my husband is the honored guest. I'm very proud of you Joseph. For everything you've accomplished and have yet to accomplish."

He nodded. Yes; he would accomplish everything he'd hoped for and more. Technically, he already had it all, but he wasn't yet satisfied. His wife deserved a castle, if that is what she wanted, and he was determined to give her everything and anything her heart could ever desire. "I will accomplish even greater things with you by my side. I'll give you everything, I'll give you the world, whether you like it or not."

She smiled, her expression telling him that she knew he spoke the truth. But Arianna was a more humble soul. She didn't require wealth to be happy, she didn't need the biggest house or the fastest car to feel special about herself. She was content living a meager life, if it meant that she had her husband.

"I'll never need those things, Joseph. All I'll ever need is you. Don't let the idea of extraordinary wealth tear you apart from me. I've seen how those high powered husbands leave their wives behind in shadows while they step out into the limelight. Don't lose yourself in your determination to shower me in money and fame. I prefer you over anything you could ever offer me."

Placing his mouth over hers, Joseph started soft, but gradually deepened their kiss until both were left breathless and panting. He wanted nothing more but to continue forward, to lay her out underneath him on the couch where they sat, but he had business to attend to - for her.

He let go of Arianna and stood suddenly, his hands hurriedly working to straighten the material of his suit. Reaching down, he grasped her hand and pulled her up beside him, chuckling when he noticed how her skirt had shifted into an awkward position around her legs. He reached over and took the material between his hands, quickly pulling it back into place. Arianna moved away from him laughing, always amused by his need to take care of her in every way.

"I have a business meeting I must attend. You should run home and start getting ready for the evening. Which dress were you planning to wear?"

"I don't know…" Her words sounded funny, her continued laughter preventing her lips from functioning properly. "I haven't thought about it. Which one do you prefer?"

She stepped behind the couch, a bright grin beaming from her face and it appeared she was daring him to go after her. Joseph straightened his spine, pulled his shoulders back and imitated a man looking over his conquest. Playing into her game, he motioned as if he would respond, but stepped forward unexpectedly grasping her wrist and pulling her from around the couch. She let out a small cry when he picked her up and placed her back against the wall.

When their combined laughter ceased, he answered, "Wear the blue one, the one that matches your eyes. I will not be the most powerful man in attendance tonight, but with you in that dress, I will most assuredly be the luckiest bastard there." His tone grew serious and his eyes burned into hers with sincerity. "I mean it, Arianna, I couldn't be the man that I am without you."

Chapter Three

Looking in the full length mirror, Arianna, turned left and then right in order to examine the sleek blue satin ball gown she wore for her husband. The material was simple perfection in the way it flowed over her body like cascading rain. Satisfied with the dress, she sat down at her dressing table and styled her hair up into a simple twist, securing the errant strands with diamond crusted pins. Applying minimal makeup, she swept on a layer of gloss over her lips just as Joseph stepped out of the bathroom dressed in his formal tuxedo.

The material clung to his body in all the right places, moving with him gracefully as he sauntered across the room. His hair was styled back and his golden cufflinks reflected the light in the room when he moved. He was the definition of debonair – his proud posture and heightened stance giving him the appearance of a powerful and brutal force. Arianna's eyes swept over the broad expanse of his chest and shoulders, her heart beating faster as she followed his form down to gaze at his narrow waist. He was as beautiful as he was intelligent and she was grateful to be his wife and to be allowed the gift of his attention and love.

"If you will be the luckiest man because of this dress, than the tuxedo you're wearing will make me the envy of every woman who is there tonight. You look stunning, Joseph – impressive as ever." She stood up to take her husband's outstretched hand and allowed him to lead her from their bedroom, through the living room and out to the waiting limousine. After the limo driver had opened the door for her, she slid into the spacious backseat of the vehicle, straightening her dress underneath her while she watched her husband crawl in beside her. Once the door was closed, Joseph grabbed two crystal flutes and a bottle of chilled champagne from a table to his side. Handing her a glass, he popped the cork from the bottle, allowing it to bounce off the privacy screen between the driver and the backseat.

"Here's a toast to a wonderful evening with the most beautiful woman in the world." He lifted his glass to her and she smiled while bouncing her glass lightly against his.

"And here's to the most wonderful husband a woman could ever ask for." She sipped from her glass and admired Joseph from over the rim, watching as his neck moved from swallowing the golden liquid. Their destination was not far and the drive only lasted thirty minutes. Within that amount of time, Joseph had ravished her as much as he could, causing her to need a moment to fix her hair before stepping out of the car.

When she finally took Joseph's hand, she was escorted from the car out onto a luxurious red carpet bordered by red ropes, keeping onlookers at a safe distance from the party attendees. The flash of camera strobes blinded Arianna while she allowed Joseph to lead her inside. She noticed how Joseph's name was called out by the press who were crushed together along the sidelines; their desperation for an interview apparent in their shouted requests. Joseph ignored them, opting instead to keep his eyes trained to Arianna at his side. She smiled up at him, proud of the man she called her husband.

Once inside, Arianna's eyes widened to see the sheer decadence of the ballroom where the party was being held. The room was not yet crowded when they arrived and she was able to look across the room at the tables elegantly set with crystal and china table settings sitting atop stark white table clothes. The interior of the ballroom was much larger than any room she'd seen and a stage was set at the front of the room. A crystal chandelier hung gloriously at the center of the room and her eyes could not look away from the iridescent light it cast along the ceiling and walls of the room. Joseph noticed her amazement and pulled her closer to him so that he could whisper in her ear.

"Do you like the chandelier? One day I will buy you a beautiful home, Arianna, and in that home will hang a chandelier just as grand, if not more so, than the one that hangs in this room. This is just the beginning my love, soon your home will be the most beautiful in existence."

26

His voice was like smooth silk against her skin and she blushed knowing her husband would follow through with his promises to lavish her in luxury and wealth. Whereas her heart sang with pride at his accomplishments and drive, her stomach twisted at the thought that Joseph would never understand that it wasn't wealth that she wanted.

Arianna had grown up in a simple family. Although, they were not as wealthy as the old money society in which Joseph had been raised, they were comfortable living with her father's income and she was taught that love should be held more valuable than any object or fanciful desire. Her parents had died before she'd even met Joseph, but their lessons still resonated in her head in the years since they'd passed.

Joseph led her to their table that sat front and center of the large room. Taking his seat at the table, Joseph appeared like a king, dignity oozing from every pore. Couples passed by, making sure to stop and make small talk with the guest of honor. Arianna was having a splendid time sipping champagne and observing her husband while he shone in his element. She would never get used to the attention they received due to his growing notoriety, but she wouldn't openly voice her concerns, not wanting to chance upsetting Joseph.

Once dinner had been finished and the attendees at the event were sipping coffee and eating dessert, Joseph was requested to give his speech at the podium on stage. When he stood,

Arianna's eyes took in her proud husband, a smile lighting her face to see him become the center of attention. She expected him to walk instantly to the stage, but he surprised her when his eyes met hers and he made it a point to walk to her side of the table, offer his hand and pull her up from her chair into an embrace and kiss straight out of a romance novel. Dipping her backwards, he kissed her with such passion that Arianna could hear the audible gasps, giggles and sighs sounding from the women throughout the room. Her husband was a true romantic and she adored every second of her time with him. Lifting her back into an upright position, he smiled brightly at her before assisting her back into her seat and turning to make his way up the stage and to the podium positioned in the center.

The room quieted down once Joseph was in his position to speak. Except for the occasional clink of a glass against a dish, a cough or the discreet clearing of a throat, no sound emanated throughout the room as Joseph prepared to discuss his acquisition of the company.

His grey eyes looked around the room, his posture was strong and assured. When he began his speech, the silence in the room somehow grew even more silent as his words reverberated off the walls and ceiling. He didn't need the podium at which he stood, because he didn't need his speech to be written out; his mind was the type that could memorize anything, no matter the length.

"I'd like to start off this evening by thanking each and every person in this room for being here tonight to congratulate me on an accomplishment not normally known by a man my age. Although, I do not view this achievement as anything that deserves recognition, I know that it is unusual for not only a single man, but one as young as me, to take over a company as large as Estate Acquisitions. I also know that many of you have questions regarding my methodology for success and the type of drive it takes for a man such as me to prevail in a business typically reserved for far more established and experienced men..." He paused, his eyes shifting down to lock with the crystal blue orbs of Arianna's. He smiled and looked away to continue his speech. "...But before I get into the intricate details of mergers and acquisitions, I must be honest in telling all of you, that without my lovely wife, Arianna, by my side, I would not have the drive to achieve my success. She is a fire that burns within my body, my heart and my soul, and, for her, I can accomplish anything..." Joseph laughed to himself at some inner thought, before once again donning the expression of a serious businessman and looking up into the expectant faces of the crowd. "...And to the gentlemen sitting here tonight – my associates, my peers, and my competitors – I'll have you know that because there is only one woman on this Earth as amazing as my wife, I have a secret weapon that you cannot acquire for yourselves, and as such, I will become a force to be reckoned with." He smiled a cruel smile, one that no person could mistake as anything but the expression of a man who knew he had everyone beat.

"Gentlemen – consider yourselves warned."

. . .

The booming sound of applause coupled with the entire room standing in ovation of her husband left Arianna breathless in her surprise at the admiration of the audience. When Joseph had stopped gushing about her, he'd immediately launched into a discussion of the myriad of tasks he had to daily accomplish in his position, his future goals for the company, and he even touched on the tenets of a business that required a ruthless skill by which any man must operate in order to compete in the industry. For the most part, Joseph's speech was the typical oration of a professional, dull in nature but expected to be said. However, there were certain parts, small phrases used and minute changes to Joseph's expression that concerned Arianna. She'd never really observed Joseph when he worked and she'd never seen him don the mask of a merciless entrepreneur, one who was intent on gaining not only money, but power in his position at the top. She tried to shake the concern, attempted to convince herself that it was standard for a person in his career, but the nagging warning of a hidden side to her husband would not stop brushing across her thoughts.

Her eyes followed Joseph as he descended the stairs. She watched his powerful swagger, a stride that not only attracted, but warned any person whose path he crossed. She scrutinized every motion of his body until he returned to their table, sitting down and once again seeming to transform back into the man she knew and loved. The abrupt change in his demeanor was staggering and when Arianna accepted his outstretched hand from across the surface of the table, she did so with the newly discovered knowledge that there were two sides to Joseph Carmichael.

An hour passed and in that time Joseph led Arianna around the large room, mingling with the guests.   Maintaining a bright smile on her face, Arianna tried desperately to be the epitome of a perfect wife, laughing with the women when they joked and cautiously tolerating the compliments of their over-attentive husbands. Having been raised in a modest family, she was unsure of the behaviors expected of her in this environment. She was surprised when she was approached by an older gentlemen who requested a dance and she looked to Joseph for instruction on her response. Joseph was buried deep in an animated conversation with a business associate so Arianna politely excused herself, remembering that Joseph had wanted her to be the most desired at the ball. She allowed the man to lead her onto the dance floor, holding her body apart from him while they danced so as not to appear improper. The man was a delightful dancer as he spun her regally throughout the room. When the lighthearted song ended, he stepped away, bowing before escorting her back to her husband. But while making their way back to where Joseph stood, Arianna noticed a darkness in Joseph's gaze. It was fleeting in its duration but it was enough to tell her that her husband was upset.

In an attempt to the shake the unease in her head, and while Arianna continued following her husband around the large room, she had allowed herself to drink one too many glasses of champagne. She was feeling slightly dizzy and was ready to call it a night and return home to bed. Joseph also seemed tired, but he was fastidious in his obligation to speak with each and every man and woman in the room before he excused himself to leave.

When, at last, it was time for the two of them to return home, Arianna was distracted by a group of ladies who wished to speak with her, while Joseph was approached by two men who Arianna did not recognize. Politely looking between the ladies and her husband, Arianna took secretive glances at the men, noticing a darker edge to their body language and expressions. At first, Joseph didn't appear to want much to do with the men, but then the taller man said something that grabbed Joseph's attention. Arianna watched as her husband pulled a business card from his wallet and handed it to the men within five minutes of their approach. After handing them the card, Joseph excused himself and made his way over to Arianna, stealing her away from the women so that he could escort her home.

The ride home was quiet for the most part; and Joseph uncharacteristically stared out his window for the majority of the trip. Given her exhaustion, Arianna didn't attempt to engage him in conversation. She was happy to avoid asking him the questions that plucked at her mind, at least until a time when she could process what she'd seen.

When they returned home and undressed from the evening, Joseph approached her as he had almost every night before, waiting and anxious to take his wife to their bed.

Picking her up in his arms, his warm mouth came down on hers, his tongue forceful in its demand for entry. She opened her mouth, allowing him to fill her with his scent and his taste, the remnants of the champagne he'd consumed earlier still noticeable on his tongue. She lost herself in that moment, suddenly reminded of why she'd fallen for the man who carried her. Laying her down on the bed, he pulled at the belt of her silken robe, baring her to his watchful eyes. Her body hummed in anticipation of his touch. He lifted her body to remove the robe from beneath her, but instead of idly tossing it aside as was his usual practice, he pulled the belt from the loops of the robe before he dropped the robe to the floor and turned back to her with an odd expression across his face.

"Would you like to play a game, beautiful?" Heat filled his eyes as he rubbed his hands up along the sides of her torso, her body quivering in response to his touch. His voice dripped with seduction as he goaded her into a response to his question.

"What kind of game?" Her responsive question was hesitant and unsure, but she trusted Joseph, and would go along with whatever he asked. She'd never denied him in the time that they'd been married and he'd never taken from her what she hadn't willingly given.

"Do you trust me?" His breath rolled along her neck as he spoke into her sensitive skin.

After Arianna nodded her consent, Joseph grabbed her arms, lifting them above her head, before he secured one end of the belt over her wrists and the other to the posts of the headboard. She attempted to wriggle free, but he'd tied the cloth too tightly to her wrists and her movement only caused the material to bind her even more.

Nervous laughter bubbled from her throat when she asked, "Joseph? What's gotten into you tonight?"

His eyes darkened as he ran his nose along her jawline, down further until his faced was nestled just above her breasts. His voice slid across her skin, cold as ice, when he answered, "I thought it wouldn't bother me to see other men staring at you hungrily while you flounced around tonight in that room. I thought it would bring me pride to know that my wife is desired above all other women..." He looked up, his eyes covered over by a sheen of what looked like anger, but the look was so foreign, Arianna couldn't be sure.

"...But instead of pride, I felt resentment; I felt a need to stab out the eyes of every man who glanced in your direction." He moved his face to softly nip at her breast and she jumped at the sudden sensation. "I never realized how possessive I've become of you, Arianna, and tonight, I intend to show you just how thoroughly you belong to me."

Chapter Four

Arianna sat on the bench in front of the piano, her fingers splayed motionlessly over the keys. As usual, she'd spent her day cleaning her home and preparing a meal for when Joseph returned from work before finally sitting down to absorb herself in her instrument. What began as a light song, one filled with the staccato sounds of airy and harmonious notes, had gradually shifted to a slower song made up of darker notes, discordant harmonies and a flat tone that spoke of despondency and despair. When she recognized the dreadful tone of the song her fingers elicited from the keys, she stopped suddenly, pulling her hands away from the instrument while tears fell down the pale skin of her face to the ivory below. Examining her wrists, she allowed her eyes to brush over the slight bruises that circled her skin where the belt had been fastened too tightly the night before.

When they'd awakened that morning, Joseph had been the first to notice the bruises. He apologized profusely and blamed the alcohol he'd consumed as the reason for his roughness when they'd made love. Arianna had stayed in bed while he'd dressed and she'd failed to escort him to the door as was their usual routine. When she'd finally managed the strength to pull herself from beneath the covers, she stopped suddenly while walking into the restroom, the mirror reflecting back to her eyes the reddened and bruised marks on her breasts and body where Joseph had bitten her.

And now, under the light of the lamp that sat above her music, those bruises and marks were made more visible; angry purples and reds violently twisting around themselves, the hint of a green discoloration dotted within. She was unsure how long she stayed there silently observing the evidence of Joseph's loss of control, but when she heard the front door open and then close, she wrenched herself from her thoughts and attempted to paste a fake smile on her face when she stood to greet her husband.

His steps were heavy as he crossed the room swiftly to take her hands into his. Like light bouncing off steel, a glint came into his eye, alerting Arianna to his rush of excitement. She smiled shyly, not yet understanding why he appeared elated.

"You'll never guess what happened today. I have to tell you everything, but baby, this news will change our lives. I met with two men at the office, they offered a deal to me that I would have been stupid to refuse." His words were difficult to understand due to the quickened pace of his speech.

He picked her up, not noticing in his haste that she'd winced from where he pressed on one of the many bruises on her body. Spinning her around, he laughed and gazed up into her face before placing her back on the floor and steadying her from falling. "Is dinner ready? I'm starving and I want to tell you about it."

Straightening her skirt, she looked up at him warily, concerned that he seemed to have forgotten what had occurred the evening before. Pushing past her hesitation, she nodded 'yes' and grasped his hand to lead him into the kitchen so that she could prepare their plates. When they finally settled at the dining room table, Arianna toyed with her food while listening to Joseph tell her about his day and his new business venture.

"And were these the same men that I saw approach you at the ball last night?"

Joseph eyed her across the short expanse of the table. Anger flitted across his brow briefly before he settled his shoulders back into a relaxed posture.

"Yes. I gave them my card and they called me in the morning to set up our conference this afternoon. Arianna, this could make us the wealthiest family in town."

"But, they're criminals, Joseph. What they are asking you to do..."

"I WON'T BE COMMITTING ANY CRIMES!!" He stood up from the table, jostling the table settings when his fists came down on top of the wood. "Why are you questioning my decision? I'm doing this for us – for you!" His anger was immediate and unexpected. Arianna jumped back in her seat, shrinking down in response to the anger in his tone. Too afraid to speak, she sat silently in her chair watching as he moved from his seat and paced the floor. This wasn't her husband, Joseph had never acted this way before.

Seemingly calmed down, he stopped pacing, but she noticed how his hands continued to clench. Her voice was soft, mouse-like, as she spoke. "Joseph, I didn't mean to question you, I just don't understand how dealing with common criminals will help your career. You're doing well enough on your own, why take a risk?"

"These men are not *common* street trash, Arianna. They are educated men. I'm doing fine, yes, but what they are offering is easy money, LOTS of easy money. Wealth beyond anything you or I have ever known. It will propel me forward ten times as fast as I'm moving now."

"But Joseph, you'll be supporting common criminals. People who are spreading death and chaos over society. I don't care if the men you spoke with are wealthy or educated, the men they support are the ones on the streets feeding drugs to children, taking the lives of innocent people, why would you even consider their offer?" She knew she should shut up, knew that he'd been acting strange since the ball, but she had to say something to introduce reason back into the mind of her husband.

His expression blank, he moved to the wall, leaning up against it while running his hand through his hair. She knew that motion, knew he was struggling with his decision. When his hand came to his face and he squeezed his temples, she realized silence was a better decision than continuing the argument. He pulled his hand away from his face and a cruel look swirled in his eyes, the shadowed grey twisting over itself like molten steel.

His voice was flat, the baritone quality deepening as he slowly stalked over to where she sat. "Do you know how sweet you are Arianna? Like an seraphim, one who exudes beauty through her innocence and music."

The words he used were nothing unusual for how he normally referred to her, but the quality to his tone frightened her.

"But, you are so naïve. You have no idea what it takes to make it in this world, to become something more than what your father had become." He turned her chair so that she faced away from the table and placed his palms down, effectively caging her against her chair. His behavior was offsetting and she was unsure what she could do. "From here on out, Arianna, I'll make the business decisions and YOU will support me in those decisions. Save your concerns for the things that you know something about...music, cooking, cleaning..." His face twisted again. "The *child* you have yet to give me."

Tears burned at the back of her eyes, but she refused to let them spring forth. His words were a hit to the stomach, the slice of steel across her heart. "Why are you acting so cruel towards me? Last night, and today? It's like you are someone else entirely. I don't understand." The sobs caught in her throat causing her voice to waiver, each syllable cracking as she spoke.

He laughed. A small chuckle at first, nothing more than the shaking of his shoulders; but that chuckle grew louder, until finally bursting forth, scaring her even more than before.

He quieted. Finally gaining his composure, he looked deep into her eyes, and guilt skittered across his expression when he recognized the fear in hers. He pulled away from her and crossed the room, his shoulders sagging when he recognized how he'd behaved.

After a few moments, he finally spoke. "Forgive me." Falling to his knees he crawled towards her, resting his head in her lap when he stopped at the base of her chair. "Forgive me. Oh God. I'm so sorry, Arianna. I didn't mean…" His words cut off and Arianna placed her hand on his head, still frightened but also concerned for the man she loved. He looked up at her before he rose to his knees, taking her face between his hands. "I've been under so much stress lately. I want to give you everything and it frustrates me that I can't provide you with everything I want as quickly as I feel I should."

Her hand reached up to brush along his cheek, the stubble scratching across her palm in her attempt to soothe his rage. "I don't need the things you insist on giving me, Joseph. I need you; my loving husband. Nothing more. Please tell me you'll reconsider having anything to do with those men. You're better than that – than them." The tears finally fell from her eyes and she could see his expression soften. Reaching up he grabbed her hand and pulled it down so that he could look over the bruises on her wrist. He flinched at the sight of the angry marks that tore across her skin. His eyes watered when he looked back up at her, confusion furrowing his brow, remorse darkening his gaze.

"Forgive me." His words were breathless and strained. "I don't know what's come over me these past couple of days. I'll reconsider, Arianna, I'll reconsider for you."

Chapter Five

Two years had passed since Joseph had taken control of Estate Acquisitions. Within those two years, Joseph had amassed a small fortune, tripling the size of the company and growing more powerful than even the most elite within his field. He'd reconsidered doing business with his newfound associates after the night he'd scared his wife, but not being able to shake the idea of the wealth they could bring, he continued his dealings in private, hiding information from her and allowing her to believe that he'd declined their offer. He felt guilty for lying to her, but he knew that her mind was not capable of the ruthless skill required for business. He also saw nothing wrong with the arrangement he'd made with the men and he'd convinced himself that his decision was well-founded when gazing on the home he was finally able to provide for his wife.

He'd allowed the men to use his company as a front to filter money in order to hide the profits of their crimes. In exchange for the use of his company, Joseph was able to keep a percentage of those funds for himself. Within a year's time, rumors spread through the underground channels regarding the success of their arrangement and more high-powered men had approached Joseph requesting that they be allowed to do the same. By the second year, Joseph no longer had to buy and sell companies to make money, thanks to the business dealings with the criminals he assisted. He tried not to think about what these men were doing and where the money was coming from, focusing instead on the growth of his wealth and his power within the community. He knew he was dealing with questionable characters, but his knowledge of their crimes was not enough to sway him from his decision.

Standing back from his newly acquired property, Joseph placed his arm around Arianna, delighted to finally give her the home he felt a woman like her deserved. The large mansion stood proudly at the center of a 100 acre piece of land. Its center was domed, the foyer and connected ballroom flanked by two large wings that ran along its sides. Each wing contained two large gourmet kitchens, multiple common areas and various apartments that acted as small homes within the building. It had once been a hotel, but Joseph had purchased the property with the intent of selling off the assets and creating a home for Arianna and himself.

"Don't you think it's a little big for us, Joseph? I'm afraid I'll get lost just trying to locate a bathroom." She joked at his side, but her attempt at levity was lost on him. He'd wanted to see her face beam at the sight of it, but instead she appeared reserved, undecided on whether she was pleased with the present he'd given her.

Annoyance laden in his tone, Joseph responded, "I thought you would be happy. There will be plenty of room for everything. I'll never have to leave the house again if I use the west wing for my business and the right as a home for you and I, and a child when we are finally successful in our attempts."

He knew he hit a nerve by bringing up their inability to conceive but he was also hurt by her lack of enthusiasm over the home he'd bought her. His need to strike out was not easily contained due his desire for an heir that had become an unending obsession hidden deep within the confines of his mind.

Arianna remained quiet and he knew she was keeping her thoughts to herself, a habit she'd developed over the few years they'd been married. A fake smile across her face, she looked up at him. "Let's go inside, maybe if I look around, its size won't intimidate me as much as it does from the view outside." It was a weak effort, but one Joseph could appreciate.

Walking her inside, he became eager to show her the best part of the mansion. Covering her eyes with his hand, he led her into the center ballroom. "Are you ready for this, my love? When I uncover your eyes, look up."

Slowly he peeled his hand from her face. Her attention immediately traveling to the ceiling and her breath leaving her in an astonished puff of air when she first saw the sophisticated and intricate design of the crystal chandelier that hung in the center of the room.

Breathlessly, she said, "Joseph..."

He smiled, placing a finger over her mouth to silence her words.   Looking deep into the boundless blue of her eyes, he said, "I promised you years ago that I would buy you a home with a crystal chandelier. This building is yours to do with as you please. I know that with your touch, it will be the envy of every person lucky enough to set eyes on it."

Arianna nodded, glancing around the room. Her eyes brushed over the gaudy floral wallpaper and the chair rails that could use a darker stain so that they matched the dark wood beams that ran in lines, converging at the ceiling's curved center. Although her annoyance with Joseph's intrepid purchase still nagged at her mind, she looked forward to redecorating, adding her personal touch to the space Joseph had chosen as their home. She was also thankful for a project of the mansion's magnitude to distract her during the long days while Joseph was at work; because, over the past few months, she'd been saddened at how Joseph had put in more hours and spent larger portions of time away.

Pushing herself up onto her toes, she kissed Joseph on the cheek, smiling earnestly up at the man who intended to give her the world. "Thank you. Where would you like me to start?"

An lustful idea flicked through his mind and he smiled slyly when he answered, "Start with our apartment at the end of the right wing. It's one of the largest suites in the entire mansion. I'll take you there now." Gripping her hand, he led her through the large wooden doors of the ballroom out into a long corridor. The sound of their steps against the stone floors echoed through the halls as they traveled the distance to their suite. Pulling a key from his pocket, Joseph unlocked the rounded double doors, pushing them forward to unveil a massive, unfurnished room. Arianna stepped inside, her eyes immediately moving over the built in bookshelves on the left of the room and the dining area and kitchen on the right.

Crossing the room, Arianna pushed open the large double doors that led into an office, her eyes traveling over the tall built in shelves. Her eyes alight with excitement, she spun towards Joseph. "Will you be working in here? Will I get to see more of you now that you can work from home?"

He chuckled. "We could make this *one* of my offices, but as I said earlier..." He strode to her, wrapping his arms around her waist, swaying her back and forth. "...I thought the west wing would be a good place to deal with business affairs. Once our child arrives, I'd like to keep the two halves of my life separate from one another. Your spirit and that of our future child will be too precious to be muddied or weighed down by the dealings of men and their money."

Arianna's brows furrowed, but she knew her husband was attempting to guard her in the only way he knew how. "Where are the bedrooms?"

A salacious smile lining his lips, Joseph winked before grabbing her hand and leading her towards the opposite set of doors across the living room. "I love how you can't wait to get working on that child." The shift in his thoughts was sudden, the vision of her beauty in the low light of the room drawing his attention, stoking his need to dominate her - to possess her.

An enchanted and melodic laugh floated through the air as Joseph dragged his unsuspecting wife through the corridor to the back bedroom. When he pushed open the doors to the master suite, Arianna gasped to see how much space was hidden within the room. She moved quickly through the unfurnished space, her hands brushing across the chair rails and textured red paint on the walls. "I love this color. Would you mind if I use it throughout the building?"

His chest pressed against her back, Joseph brought his mouth to her ear, lightly sucking on the sensitive lobe before responding, "Promise me to make our home as beautiful as you, and you can use any color you like." Joseph observed his wife, his pants tightening in response to the sudden onslaught of erotic images of her in his head. He could care less if she wanted to paint the entire house green at that moment, his pride creating within him a masculine desire to stalk and conquer the woman in his arms.

His hands smoothed down the sides of her body, causing her to tremble against his skin. Her breath caught when he aggressively took her hand, pulling her into the large connected bathroom. "Are you feeling dirty, my love? Perhaps a shower would benefit us both." Seduction dripping thick from his words, his eyes moved over her body, a fire sparking within him after he focused on the soft curves hidden beneath the modest clothes that she wore.

She turned to him, surprise touching her features; but before she could voice her reply, Joseph covered her mouth with his hand, backing her towards the sunken shower at the corner of the room. With her back pressed heavily against the glass wall, he put his mouth to her ear, enjoying the way her body responded to the whisper of his breath against her skin. Reality shifted and his basic drive took over. His need for her at that moment went beyond love, beyond anything that could be considered sweet or romantic. It was a driving, carnal desire that made every muscle in his body tense, that caused his blood to forcefully surge through his veins. Holding her motionless against the wall, he was quiet for a few moments before finally saying, "You are mine, Arianna, never forget that. You'll never have to be away from me again. I've given you a home and a piece of land that will provide you with everything you will ever need."

"Am I trapped here, Joseph? Is that your intent?" Her words were spoken in jest but a grain of truth was buried within the question.

Softly, his chest rumbled against her, his humor towards an inner thought made apparent by the movement of his body and the twist to his lips. "Such a sweet and beautiful creature you are." His finger reaching up to softly slide along her cheek, his grey eyes locked to the cobalt starbursts within hers. "You've been trapped since the day I met you, but if it is my intentions that concern you, just know that the only plan I have at this moment is to take your naked body in every way possible, over every solitary inch of this home."

His teeth found the sensitive skin just beneath her ear while his hands slid along her back, drawing the zipper of her dress down until resting just above the curve to her ass. As the material fell from her shoulders, flowing gracefully down along her torso, his lips followed along, nipping at the sensitized flesh, his tongue flicking out to take in the salt taste of her skin.

When the dress finally pooled at her feet, he caged her against the walls with his arms. His forehead pressed against hers, he demanded, "Undress me, Arianna."

With eyes the color of fiery mercury, he watched as her slender fingers worked over the buttons of his shirt, each one opening to expose his heated skin to the cool air in the room that wound itself between their bodies. Her fingernails clicking against each other, his heart beat harder at the thought of the feel of those nails trailing down his back. He covered her body with his while she worked lower, finally freeing him of his pants before reaching up again to push his shirt off his strong shoulders.

Quietly he led her down the steps into the shower. Flicking on the water, she shouted out when the frigid temperature met with her skin, the tips of her breasts instantly hardening into points that he took no time covering with his mouth and hand. Shoving her against the stone tiled wall, his hands gripped her legs, roughly pulling her legs around his waist before violently spearing himself inside the warm heat of her body.

Driving himself within her, his teeth clamped down where the skin of her neck met her shoulder. She cried out, her body shuddering against him while the muscles of her core milked him hungrily of everything he had to give her. Forcing her towards a painful peak, his hand reached up to grip her around her neck, just below the line of her jaw. With his mouth pressed against hers, he demanded, "Tell me who owns you, Arianna; tell me to whom you belong."

Her lips parted, her breath stolen by the beat of his body against hers. A disjointed whisper, she responded, "You, Joseph...I belong to you."

A final assault inside her and they both screamed out their release, the water cascading around them, the steam of its heat coloring their skin. His forehead fell down on hers once more when he peeked at her from underneath his water soaked lashes.

"Yes, Arianna – and you must never forget it."

Chapter Six

Three years passed since Arianna and Joseph had moved into the mansion that quickly became not only their home, but a popular gathering place for the elite members of society. Balls and other parties were held in their home every week, and Joseph and Arianna became the wealthiest couple within their social circle. Joseph was now twenty-nine years old and had become even more powerful within the community of criminals and thieves whose crimes secretly funded his business.

However, Joseph was a man who obsessed over power; one who could not sit idly by as other men managed the dealings of the networks that fed his wealth. Curiosity and the need to rule eventual led Joseph further into the activities of the crime networks of which he'd become a part. Drugs, weapons, murder, espionage and prostitution...it didn't matter, as long as his pockets were lined, Joseph was able to shake off the loss of morality that came with his position. When he'd learned the trade well enough, he systematically secured control over the different networks, discovering that enough money could buy the quiet death of an associate;

and, naturally, once that associate had been destroyed, the men that worked underneath him would then swear allegiance to Joseph. Never having the actual blood on his hands, Joseph was able to convince himself that what he did was done to support his wife, to provide her with wealth beyond comprehension, rather than as a result of his driving need to rule.

He ran his network utilizing the same skills required to take over Estate Acquisitions when he'd been younger, taking over different criminal organizations and consolidating them into multiple areas of crime specialties and subdividing those specialties into units. Referring to the network, simply as "The Estate," Joseph then demanded that those units work together to continuously increase profit and take over larger areas within the country. Joseph was nothing if not a genius in business, legitimate or otherwise; and eventually, he'd organized a system of crime so sophisticated, the few authorities who questioned his activities were quickly paid off to remain quiet, or killed before they could cause problems. Within a year, Joseph had most of the police force and other government agencies on his payroll, securing the ability for his men to operate without concern of being caught.

A typical consequence of Joseph's status within the shady dealings of the criminal networks he'd grown to control was the bitter and sometimes violent rivalries between Joseph's network and other networks whose *businesses* were being run to ground. He'd recruited one man in particular who he trusted above all else to oversee a security detail around the grounds of the mansion. Connor was not only an intelligent man who reminded Joseph of himself, but was also a savage fighter, one Joseph knew could control the lesser criminals within the network. Without Arianna's knowledge, Connor was always on the grounds, living in the west wing and supervising the operations of the network while Joseph was off tending to his wife.

Ever protective of Arianna, Joseph kept to his promise of limiting his business dealings to the west wing. When they'd first moved in, he'd allowed her to enter the wing in order to decorate the rooms; but, eventually he'd demanded that she never enter that wing for fear that she'd learn the truth of the men who worked for him and served him. She was allowed as far as the ballroom, but was restricted from traveling beyond that large, domed room. Keeping her separate from his business was not easy and he lied often; however, the building was so large that Arianna never noticed the men who came and went; the private entrances practically ensuring there would never be a chance that she would answer a door or run into his associates in the halls.

In their suite, the small office that Joseph had spent many hours in at first, eventually came to rest under a thin layer of dust from its lack of use. It took two years for Arianna to finally complete her changes to the mansion, but when she'd finished, she found herself succumbing to a depressive ennui as a result of the solitude brought about by her and Joseph's long hours apart.

Still without a child, Arianna spent her days wandering the right wing of the mansion. She'd turned a smaller suite into a music room and spent most of her waking hours in that room composing music that she'd play for Joseph during the late evening hours when he returned to her side. He'd always appear haggard at first, the smell of smoke and alcohol often clinging to his clothes, and the more time that passed, the longer it would take for her to coax him back into the normal demeanor of the man that she'd married. She knew how his mind worked, his obsessive need for more power, more wealth, more...control. It had been subtle in the beginning, but the longer she lived with him, the more she noticed the instability of his moods and his fitful nights spent pacing the floors when he was unable to shut down his thoughts to sleep.

Their relationship had become strained through the years and Arianna resented the man who appeared to only want to spend time with her when he had needs to be met. She was a body for his pleasure, a trophy to be polished and shown off during the parties and balls he'd demanded be held in their home. His love of her had turned obsessive at times, throwing him into fits of rage if he entered the right wing in search of her and couldn't find her as easily as he would've liked. It was a gradual process, but one that brushed across her thoughts every night her husband returned to their suite.

On one particular morning, while sitting at the keyboard of the shining, black grand piano that Joseph had bought to be a centerpiece of her music room, Arianna toyed with the keys, her boredom affecting her ability to connect with even her music that morning. Standing up, she moved fluidly to the large bay window of the room, her eyes looking out over the woods that surrounded the house. It was still early enough that a dense fog clung to the ground, appearing like a swirling pool of mist over the leaves and small plants spread across the forest floor. She admired the thin splinters of light that broke through the thick canopies of the trees and she decided to explore the grounds around the perimeter of the house. She returned to her quarters and selected a coat that would be thick enough to guard her against the chill in the air.

When she'd finally traveled the long distance to the side doors of the corridor, she pushed out into the open air, breathing deeply, the feeling of ice blanketing her chest and lungs. The steam of her breath billowed out in front of her as she walked a path into the interior of the forest. She walked for half an hour, noticing that the path traveled parallel to the house, rather than leading her out deep into the woods. The serenity and peace of her surroundings soothed her tired spirit, energy seeping into her heart and mind from the lack of walls surrounding her.

Walking leisurely, she listened to the bird songs and the wind as it forced its way through the heavy boughs of the trees. If ever there was Heaven on Earth, Arianna thought she had found it in that moment and it had been her husband who'd given it to her. She smiled a sad smile. Their love was bittersweet because, when they were together, nothing else in the world mattered; but when they were apart, she couldn't help but feel terrified that Joseph wouldn't return the same man that he'd been when he left her in the morning.

A loud snap sounded behind her and Arianna turned suddenly, the clear blue of her eyes deliberately traveling over the distant trees and shrubs, seeking out the cause for the noise. Although the sun should have been higher in the sky, it seemed the fog had grown even more dense during the passing morning, effectively diminishing her vision to within fifty feet of her on either side. Another soft rustle and her eyes shot to her left, scanning intently seeking out the source of the sound. Her heart rate slowly sped in her chest, and her billowed breath appeared before her at a more frequent rate. She'd walked such a distance that she was unsure where on the property she stood, but she was comforted to find that, in the distance, she could still make out the lights of the mansion. The next snap that she heard had her eyes shooting back in the direction from which she'd traveled. She stepped backwards, unsure of where to run if an animal was sneaking up to attack her.

An eerie silence fell over the forest, her eyes moving desperately to locate the cause of the sounds she'd heard. When another soft wisp echoed through the trees, she looked out again, her eyes finally settling on the blonde fur of a distant deer. She laughed, her hand going to her chest in an attempt to settle the pounding beat of her heart. She watched as the deer bent down to eat plants on the ground. The animal's beauty was breathtaking. Majestically, it moved through the trees, its large antlers casting shadow when it traveled through the sparse bits of light that leaked through the thick canopies. Fascinated by its presence, she watched silently as it moved through the fog, but eventually it moved so deep into the woods that she could no longer make out its form.

Spinning on her heel, she turned to go back to the house but suddenly found herself locked within the thick arms of a strange man. His hand covered her mouth when he brought his mouth down to her ear. "And what do we have here? You appear to be lost, little one."

Forcing her off the path, he dragged her into a dark area where light could not penetrate. She felt the rough bark of a tree when he pressed her against it, his hand quickly moving to reach under her jacket and shirt. When his fingers brushed across the bottom of her breast, she opened her mouth to draw in one of his fingers, biting down hard enough to break the skin, her mouth instantly filling with the bitter, metallic taste of his blood.

The man pulled away as soon as she bit him, but brought the back of his hand across her cheek with such force, her head was knocked sideways against the rough surface of the tree. She slid down against the tree, her skin scraping across the bark and the taste of her own blood now mixing with that of the man she'd bitten.

"You like to play rough, do you?" Kneeling down he grasped her by the collar of her jacket pulling her up so that his face was nose to nose with hers. "I can play rough too." His breath smelt of cigarette smoke and liquor and when she went to scream again he covered her mouth with his yellowed fingers, careful to put enough pressure against her lips to prevent her from biting him again. His large body pressed down over her, his other hand pulled at the material of her jacket, eventually working its way towards the button of her pants. She brought her knee up, connecting weakly with his crotch, alerting him to the fact that she was intent on fighting against him.

Easily flipping her over, he used his hand to push her face down into the sodden ground, pulling at the waist of her pants and exposing her bare ass to the chilled air. She cried when his hand slipped beneath her panties, tearing the fabric in his rush to violate her.

She could barely breath, the dirt from the ground filling her nostrils and throat from her rapid inhalation of air. The skin of her cheek stung from where it had been scratched open against the trunk of the tree and then forced into the earth. Tears fell from her eyes leaving muddied trails through the dirt that now covered her face. His large hands undoubtedly bruised her skin and when he finally had her stripped off her pants, he lifted her hips towards him, letting go only briefly so that he could free himself of his pants as well.

Taking the split second of opportunity, Arianna turned her head to the side and screamed with every bit of breath she had left in her. The man instantly corrected his error, grabbing her by the hair before he forced her face back into the damp ground to silence her cries. Her mouth filled quickly with mud and her body fought against the barrier preventing her ability to breathe. Just as the man had positioned himself to force himself inside, her body tensed in her last defense against the violent intrusion. When it was clear she would be raped, Arianna heard a loud and unexpected crack above her just before the man's weight disappeared from her back. Turning her head, she spit out the mud that filled her mouth, exhaling from her nose forcefully to clear her nasal passages.

The clear blue of her eyes peeked open and fell on the shadowed blur of two men fighting just before she noticed the quickened burst of sunlight bouncing off a large metal blade. The larger of the two men swiftly overtook the smaller, the blade in his hand sinking into the skin of the other's neck, moving sideways with such force, his head slid effortlessly from his shoulders and to the unforgiving ground below.

The larger man stood straight again, his fist relaxing and releasing the body of the smaller man so that it fell to the ground, almost soundlessly. Arianna trembled, but was frozen in her fear, unable to move away from him as he approached. Kneeling down, the man rested his hand against her back.

"Are you hurt badly? Can you move?" His voice was a low baritone, the quality of it soft, yet apprehensive. "Mrs. Carmichael, can you speak?"

Confusion flooded her mind at his knowledge of her name. Adrenaline coursing a furious torrent through her veins, a tunnel threatened her vision from the assault of the chemical within her body. She attempted to shake her head, to move away from the unfamiliar man that spoke to her. Recognizing her fear towards him, the man removed his hand and put distance between them so as not to cause her more alarm.

Looking away from her, he called out to someone in the distance, instructing the unseen man to find Joseph.

Pain slowing her movement, Arianna cautiously pushed herself up from the ground, her eyes remaining focused on the man kneeling down beside her. She pulled up her pants immediately, ashamed to have been seen practically naked by a stranger. Unable to stand fully, she backed herself against a tree, her head lulling to the side in opposition to her attempts to remain conscious. She wanted to run, wanted to escape the unknown person who, just seconds before, she'd watched take another life brutally and without hesitation or shame.

Her eyelids felt heavy and her head throbbed painfully from the rush of blood through her body. Each beat of her heart echoed inside her skull as the flesh on her cheek burned under what felt like fire held to her skin. Her head weakly lulled sideways, allowing her eyes to meet with the larger stretch of sunlit ground that illuminated the entryway onto the forested path on which she sat. The man beside her remained quiet but she noticed out of her periphery vision how he stood immediately when the sunlit path that she watched became shadowed by the body of her husband and the two men who ran behind him.

Joseph ran to her quickly, his hands immediately examining her body in search of injuries. When his eyes fell on the scraped side of her face, a dark sheen of anger flooded his steel grey eyes.

"Arianna..." His voice was controlled, a lethal edge to the one word he was able to vocalize. Picking her up, he cradled her to his chest and spun quickly to exit the forest. The black tunnel continued to threaten her mind and the last thing she saw as Joseph carried her out from beneath the canopy of the trees was three men who silently walked in a triangular formation behind Joseph as he approached the mansion.

Chapter Seven

"She'll come around, Joseph. I'm sure your wife loves you enough to understand the decisions you've made for her. She's living a lifestyle unknown by the majority of the ladies in her society. She is the envy of every woman who knows her."

Joseph sat back in his leather chair, his eyes locked to those of his most trusted man across the expanse of the large wooden desk between them. His voice was regretful when he responded, "But am I responsible for what happened yesterday in the woods? If she'd known, if she *stayed* where she was supposed to stay, she wouldn't have been attacked. There's nothing I can do now but be honest with her. She'll want to leave, she'll never understand that my choice was made for her, to give her everything she could ever want."

Connor nodded his head in understanding. "Have you had the opportunity to explain? Have you ensured her that she will be protected heavily from this point forward? It will not happen again, I won't allow it."

Steel grey met emerald green when Joseph looked straight into the loyal eyes of his guard. A shrewd intelligence filled the grey, his knowledge that Connor would not falter or fail apparent in his gaze. "You are to remain at her side at all times. I trust you to oversee her daily activities, to make sure that no other man amongst your team comes in contact with her." Sitting back, he folded one hand over the other, resting his chin on the tops of his enjoined hands while considering what he would divulge to his wife. "I haven't spoken to her yet, she slept most of the night, only waking occasionally to some bastard nightmare from which I could not protect her. I had a nurse come to the mansion this morning to tend to her wounds. I wanted to give her some time before I explained."

Nodding again, Connor relaxed into his chair. "I'll go with you when you explain. It might make her more receptive to my presence."

Joseph chuckled darkly, knowing full well that his modest wife, a soul who would never cause or allow harm to another, could never understand the shady dealings he'd undertaken over the years. "She'll resist. She may seem weak, but there is more to her than can easily be seen. However, she is also smart enough to know she has no choice but to remain where she can be kept safe. Every demon out there now knows my name, knows that if there is any weakness in me at all that can be attacked or exploited, it's her."

Pushing himself up from his chair, Connor paced the ground in Joseph's office. "I won't be able to manage the network while protecting her. Who will you choose to take over my responsibilities...to protect you in my absence?"

Joseph sighed loudly in response to Connor's question. "I thought about that long and hard last night while I watched over Arianna as she slept. I believe Emory can take over for the time being. It won't be often that he'll have control over the network...only at night and other times when I'm with her."

Connor stopped suddenly, and with his hands folded behind his back, he looked up at Joseph. "Are you sure? Emory seems like a loose cannon. He's good at his job, yes, but I'm not sure he can be trusted. There is something – off – about him."

Shrugging off Connor's concern, Joseph pushed himself up from his chair before saying, "I understand what you're saying, and that is the exact reason Emory has not been chosen to protect my wife. However, I believe that he can be easily handled in other matters. I've already set him on the task of determining the identity of the man who attacked Arianna. Once we discover his identity, I've instructed Emory to form a team to track down and kill whatever group it was that sent him. If he's successful in his task, I'll have no concerns as to his loyalty to The Estate and his ability to manage the men." Walking briskly towards the door, Joseph motioned for Connor to follow. "I guess it's time to talk to Arianna."

. . .

"I can't believe you've kept this hidden from me all these years, Joseph. I...why...how dare you?!" Her sobs accented her words, her voice strong, but broken by the information her husband had just revealed. "It's like I've never known you at all. This isn't you; you're a businessman, not a criminal. How does something like this happen?" Arianna turned away from her piano, spinning on the bench so that she could look her husband directly in his eyes.

Joseph stepped towards her, his hands reaching as if to touch her, but fisting instead when he pulled them back to his side. "Don't question my decisions, Arianna. You've lived a life of luxury unlike anything you've ever known before because of MY decisions..."

"Yes, Joseph, I am living a life I've never known before – you are at least correct on that! All I've ever known is love, companionship, a family who I spent time with; but now, and over the many years you've kept me *trapped* here, all I've known is solitude, sadness, a great and heartfelt longing for the husband I married years before. And now? Now, I can't even walk the grounds of the home you've given me without fear of being assaulted by the trash you've attracted into our lives. Years ago you told me you'd reconsidered their offer, you've LIED to me all this time, leaving me in the pitch black of shadow – easy prey to the lifestyle *you've* led."

Her voice dropped low, quiet and troubled as she made her next statement. "I was almost raped, Joseph...raped! Do you understand what you've done? What you've become?!"

Joseph remained still as Arianna approached him. With their eyes locked, he kept his expression blank, attempting to hide the seething rage her words had created within him.

"I want to leave, Joseph. I want to leave this place and these people, and that man who stands behind you." Her hand raised, she pointed over Joseph's shoulder towards Connor where he leaned against the wall of the music room. "Did you see what he did in those woods? How he killed that man without thought?"

His voice dripping with barely controlled wrath, Joseph said, "He was protecting YOU. That man he killed was trying to rape you, to harm you on the grounds of OUR home! You can't leave, Arianna. I love you too much to allow that."

She stilled, her sullen eyes dropping to the floor before lifting once again to look fearlessly into the molten and angry steel color of her husband's. "The way you treat me, leaving me alone most of the time, only to show up when you want sex, you call that love? That's not love, Joseph. It stopped being love years ago. What will you do if I leave? If you love me so much, will you let me go?"

"No." His response was instantaneous and assured; the deep growl of his voice a warning given to the woman he loved. "If you leave, I will drag you right back. Your family is gone, lost a long time ago, you have nowhere to go."

Something snapped within Joseph at that moment; the knowledge that his wife wanted to leave him, that she dared question his love for her, caused a violent change within his psyche. He knew she'd never understand, but never had he believed that she would choose to live without him. She was his and had been since the moment he'd laid eyes on her. He'd worked tirelessly to give her everything, but yet, she couldn't appreciate the long hours he'd worked, the tangled web of genius he'd employed to create the sophisticated network that supported them. He wouldn't allow it – he'd make her love him again.

"Connor – leave us."

Arianna's eyes left Joseph to watch as the strange man behind him pushed off the wall and strode heavily through the door of the music room, closing it behind him as he entered the hall.

"Is that man my new babysitter? Must I drag a killer around with me now just to survive the situation you've created?" She knew her words would anger him, she could see the rage burning behind his eyes, but she held strong, her nerves already shredded, her world already destroyed. She didn't fear what else she could lose now that it felt like she'd already lost all that she'd ever had.

Joseph didn't respond to her, the normally tan skin of his face turning an angry shade of red. Unbridled fury coursed violently through his face as he took determined steps towards her. She backed up, each step in perfect timing with his.

Fear suddenly brushing across her mind, she attempted to soothe the beast her husband had become. "Joseph? What are you doing? I'm sorry, I didn't mean to yell..."

"Don't apologize, Arianna." His voice was eerily calm. "You're only telling me what you really think." His head tilted to the side, his keen eyes surveying the myriad of expressions that raced across the beautiful face of his wife. "I just find it – *upsetting* – that you choose to blame me alone."

Her back against a wall, Arianna attempted in vain to keep fear from saturating her voice when she responded. "Who else do I have to blame? I didn't choose a life of crime. I didn't have an obsessive need for more money, more power. All I wanted was a loving husband, a happy home – children..."

He smiled, menace shadowing and making the expression even more cruel than Joseph had intended. It was a look she'd not seen before, one that startled her into silence as soon as it stretched across his face. "Children. Yes, Arianna. Point out the failure you've accomplished in the years we've been together. How fitting that you bring up the one thing you refuse to give me while I work endlessly to give you everything you've ever wanted."

"I don't want the things you give me! I don't care about the money, about the parties, about the prestige or the envy! All I ever wanted was you! Why can you not see that?!" She pleaded with him, her desperation dowsing her words as she cried. "I love you Joseph, but I will not remain in the life you have chosen. End this now, or let me go!"

His arms came up to cage her against the wall, the motion of his body slow and controlled while his weight pressed against her. She turned her head to the side, refused to look up into the eyes of a man who was fast becoming another stranger in her life.

His breath rolled down her cheek and the hair at the back of her neck stood on end. A feral energy rolled off Joseph in waves, causing her skin to prickle and her chest to expand from her quickened breath. A silence, pregnant with regret, shame, anger and loss, hung over them like a thick winter blanket. A man and his wife, two people who'd lived and breathed for each other only a few years before, now stood on a precipice carved out of lies and doubt, utter sadness and sudden understanding of what had become of an envied couple, of two lovers who at one time had needed each other to survive.

When Joseph's eyes closed, when his breathing deepened and Arianna looked up into the pained face of her husband, her heart melted. Pain, unforgiving and true, touched his features, caused his skin to grow pale over the sharp peaks of his cheekbones. He was tired, of that he'd not lied – and he was fighting against something she could not recognize. However, even with exhaustion weighing down his strong shoulders, she could tell that whatever he fought against carried a deep-seated resentment towards her. With tears falling from her wide-opened eyes, she reached up, her love making it impossible for her to keep from providing comfort to the man who at that moment had torn her heart, her entire world, apart. He was lost to something she didn't know, a poison that had somehow weaved itself around him, forming a cage of conspiracy and deceit, enslaving him to a lifestyle that would drive a brilliant mind mad.

The skin of her palm slid against the rough skin of his cheek, and almost instantly on that contact, his grey eyes shot open, veins of black formed from emotions so disturbing, she could barely stand to keep her eyes open long before letting her lids fall tight to her face.

Her lips falling apart, she pled, "Please, Joseph. Let me leave."

Consumed in silence that threatened to suffocate her, silence that began to push and pull at every nerve within her body, she waited to find out what Joseph would do next. But then, just barely, she heard the click of metal against metal, the soft push of a door moving against air.

The low baritone of an unsure voice sounded next. "I apologize for interrupting, but I've been informed that Emory has returned. Joseph, you may want to speak with him immediately. The information he's discovered..." Connor paused, seemingly unsure how much he could reveal with Arianna in the room. "...it's information you'll want to know right away."

Allowing her eyes to open again, she was stunned to discover that Joseph's eyes were still locked tight on her face. A mask of indifference now covered his features, the angry black veins in his eyes muted by Connor's interruption; but he never looked away from her when he answered his guard.

"I'll be there in a moment. Leave us."

Drowning in a torrential flood of pain and doubt, Arianna stood waiting for what Joseph would say or do next. Realization crept across her thoughts, the loss of hope and the knowledge that everything she thought she'd known, everything she thought they'd been, had been a lie. As if she'd been a dreamer finally waking from a long sleep, she allowed her mind to quickly travel through the past, to recognize the signs she'd ignored over the years they'd been married. Blaming herself, she thought about how she'd accepted that it had been his long hours that had been the blame for his restlessness, but the truth now slapping her in the face, she realized her husband had fallen and she'd been too ignorant to pull him back.

He stood motionless around her, the heat of his body, his scent, bathing her as she waited – the broken promise and the reminder of who her husband had been was dangled before her in that moment, a dream she would never capture again. He looked like Joseph, smelled like him, carried the same unspoken power and assurance – but he was no longer the man she'd believe him to be.

His jaw ticked, and when his sculpted lips finally opened, his voice brushed against her, seductive as silk, while, at the same time, sharp as the most lethal of blades.

The words spoken were so slow, so frightfully controlled, that there was no doubt they were the undeniable truth. "When I married you, and on our wedding night, I promised you two things, Arianna – that you were mine and that I would do whatever was necessary to give you everything you could ever want." His eyes closed as he winced, his face appearing to battle against pain of the thoughts pounding against his skull. "I have not broken those promises, so do not break yours. Do not threaten to leave me again. There is no where on this Earth that you could run, that I would not hunt you down, find you, and drag you back here, *chained* if need be, to where you belong."

His eyes opened.

"You are mine and I will not allow you to leave. While I'm gone, I will leave Connor to watch over you. He is loyal to me and will prevent any escape you attempt if you are foolish enough to try. There is no escape from me, Arianna. You WILL accept what I have done."

Pushing himself away from her, he looked her over for only a moment longer, before soundlessly turning away, disappearing out the door into the hall. Sliding to the ground, Arianna huddled over herself and grabbed her knees, rocking back and forth like a mother would do to soothe a frightened child.

Chapter Eight

His tan face was shadowed by black stubble, short and thick, creating canyons out of the cheeks of his face. An odd look to his eyes, Joseph swore he saw calculated insanity behind the gaze of the man who'd just revealed to him that a unit within his own network had been responsible for the attack on his wife.

"Do they believe they can best me so easily, that I would not have eventually discovered their plans? How many within the group took part and do we know for a fact that Arianna had been their intended target?"

Emory settled into the wing-backed chair that had been earlier occupied by Connor. "It is a simple battle for control, Joseph. These men will employ the same techniques you used to gain your seat in this network, unless of course you are quick to show them to what lengths you will go to protect it." A deeper meaning and ill intent hung on his words. "Their intended target is not of concern; only that it was an attack on *your* house. As far as I could discover, there are eleven men total who had taken part and those men have been apprehended and held until you can decide what is to be done about them."

"And what do you suggest I do about these men? Wouldn't it be simple enough to kill them and return their bodies back to those who may have supported them?"

"You could do that – or..."

Joseph's craned his neck sideways, attempting to work out the knot that had formed in the muscle. "Or, what?

"You could make an example out of them. Show any would-be traitors *exactly* how far you are willing to go to protect everything you've worked so tirelessly to build. These were criminals before you took them and shaped them into the wealthiest men in this State. But now, it seems, some believe they no longer need you. I suggest you show them how wrong they were in their belief."

Joseph considered Emory's words and agreed that swift force would be required in this situation. It was a line he'd not crossed before, but what did he have to lose? The only thing he cared about was his wife and she'd already betrayed him by allowing herself to even consider leaving his side.

"Have they confessed?"

"Does it matter?"

Each man looked at the other, a weighted question unanswered out loud, but decided, nonetheless.

Joseph sighed. "Then I will end this quickly."

Emory smiled.

Standing from his chair, Joseph paced the floors of his office. His white shirt pulled tight across his shoulders, the material abrasive against skin heated in rage.

"Call a meeting in the ballroom for this evening. I want the top men in each of the units in attendance. After tonight, there will be no doubt what will occur to any man who dares attack The Estate – from outside or from within."

"Is Connor to attend?"

"Yes."

"And who will guard your wife?"

Joseph thought silently for a moment before finally turning to Emory. A wicked smile stretching lazily across his face, he answered, "Have Connor bring her as well."

. . .

Muscles stretched taut across her back and neck, Arianna stopped rocking when her body finally quivered in revolt against the continued movement. Her tears had long ago dried up, her burning eyes only daring to peek up at the man standing across the room every once in a while. Hours had passed, but she hadn't moved, hadn't spoken, hadn't wanted to accept the company of a man she knew killed easily and without hesitation or regret. Noticing that he never looked at her directly, she eventually found herself watching him, losing her fight against her curiosity of the identity of the man and how he'd come to work for her husband. It was a small, and most likely, unimportant question, that danced amongst the countless others she had regarding Joseph.

Standing sentinel, Connor was motionless in front of Arianna, absolutely silent in his observation, while he leaned against a wall near the door to the music room. He was dressed in head to toe black, his shoulders and chest straining against the stretched material of his shirt, his pants hanging off slender hips before bulging out from the muscles in his thighs. He wore his hair short, but even still glints of light appeared to be swallowed by the ebony black strands that covered his head. He appeared younger than Joseph, but only by a few years. His face was chiseled, his strong jaw twitching every once in a while, giving away the fact that he was not, in fact, the unmoving statue that he appeared to be.

She didn't want to move, didn't know what to think of the unknown man who'd watched over her since her husband had left her crumpled on the music room floor. But she knew she could not remain there waiting for Joseph's return; knew that it would not be until the late evening hours that he'd travel back to her wing – to her.

Uncurling from her balled position on the floor, she stretched her legs out in front of her and allowed her head to fall heavily against the wall at her back.   After gaining an upright position, she watched him for a few more minutes, impressed in his ability to remain as still, as terrifyingly silent as he was.

Suddenly annoyed, she cautiously pushed herself up into a standing position, not sure if she was allowed to leave the room, or if she was trapped there until Joseph decided to return. Hesitantly, she took several steps towards the door, noticing how the man her husband had left behind finally turned when she'd approached. His eyes met hers; she stopped moving and was thoroughly entranced by the deep, multi-hued green. Perfectly contrasted by the deep tan of his skin and the silk black of his hair, the man's eyes glittered like priceless jewels, the color beaming outwards, making them appear alien and unreal. How someone of such beauty could also be a stone-cold killer was beyond her, but she knew she stared into the face of a demon, one who lurked beneath the cloak of an angel.

Stepping into the hall, she walked toward her suite, distinctly aware of the soft thud of boots behind her. For each step she took, one was matched, and she stopped suddenly to discover that those quiet thuds stopped as well. Taking another step, she heard one that followed, and she stopped again. Turning slightly, she peeked out from behind a golden curtain of hair to see that the man stood silently in wait of her next move.

"Oh! This is just ridiculous." Throwing up her hands, she marched again in the direction of her suite and she couldn't be sure, but she thought she heard a soft chuckle behind her.

Throwing open the doors, she quickly strode into the living room of her suite, flinging the doors closed behind her. Not hearing the familiar click of metal against metal, the pound of the wooden doors reverberating through the walls, she turned to find the man standing in the doorway, one door held open in each hand, and no expression in the emerald green eyes that shown brilliantly against his tanned skin.

"Am I not allowed to be in my own apartment by myself?!"

She found the man's ability to appear motionless disturbing. Her heart raced with anger and resentment, and her eyes remained locked to his face, searching for any outward sign that would betray his thoughts.

When he didn't speak, didn't move, didn't so much as flinch a muscle in response to her question, she backed into the kitchen and reached behind her to find and move a chair out from the table so that she could sit down. She kept her eyes trained on the man. A few minutes passed, crystal blue staring into emerald green, the man finally stepped forward, softly clicking the doors shut behind him, before leaning back against the wood.

The silence between them was thick, aggravating in its duration, but when his lips moved and his voice softly brushed across her senses, she flinched, not expecting the sudden sound.

"Are you afraid of me?"

An odd question. Of course she was afraid of him. Not even twenty-four hours before, she'd watched him come into the woods dressed in shadow, had seen how easily he removed a man's head without so much as a struggle.

It was only because she forced strength into her voice that she was able to speak. "Yes. I'd prefer that you leave."

Almost apologetically, he responded, "I can't leave. I've been ordered to watch over you."

"Why?"

Silence again. His eyes closing slowly, the black night of his lashes barely covering the light of his forest green eyes before opening again as he answered, "I've been asked by your husband to protect you. To ensure that no person can attempt to harm you again. He is ... concerned ... for your welfare."

Laughter shook her shoulders, the hysterical type that had no footing in actual humor, but sprang forth from anger, resentment and fear. "Is he really concerned for my welfare? Or is he concerned that I'll leave him, seek shelter in a home not overrun by criminals?" She grew quiet for a moment, her head falling into her hands but then lifted again to look indignantly into the face of the man. "Are you a criminal as well? One of the men that corrupted a good man, convinced him to lie to his wife?"

"I was hired by Joseph after The Estate had already become…what it is. My specialty is in security and defense."

"Death – that's what you mean, that is your *specialty*. I saw what you did, how easily…" Her sobs choked out her words, the honey blonde of her hair falling forward as she hid her face in her hands.

Finally when she'd pushed past the threatened tears in her eyes, she looked up again. The cobalt blue twinkling from a mixture of the lights in the room reflecting across the unshed tears. Slowly, methodically, she spoke. "He told me you would watch me to make sure I cannot leave. If I were to try, would you…"

"I'd prevent you from leaving. It wouldn't be safe, but for more reasons than you assume. Your husband loves you."

"My HUSBAND does not LOVE me! If he loved me, he'd be here by my side. There wouldn't be any need for your protection and for his continued absence. We were fine before we came to this place – HAPPY. But now… now he's lost to something that I cannot even fully comprehend. What is he supporting? Drugs? Murder? What?!"

He didn't answer; the tick of his jaw, the only sign that he'd heard her question at all.

She blinked up at him, not surprised by his lack of response. "Of course, you won't answer me. Why am I not surprised that a criminal won't admit to his acts? I must assume you are all the same."

On shaky legs, she stood up from the chair. "Am I allowed to dress by myself or do I have to sacrifice my dignity as well? Has my husband fallen so far that he'd allow another man to look over me while I'm naked?"

The corner of his lip twitched, allowing the faint outline of a dimple to grace the rough skin of his cheek.

"I will only remain in the apartment when you are here. I will not follow you when you need privacy. Joseph wouldn't appreciate or request such diligence on my part. You remain his wife, one who is protected above all else."

"Good, then I intend to spend a lot of time in my room, away from you."

He pulled his expression back to one of disinterest, effectively concealing his thoughts. "That is your choice."

She took a step towards her bedroom and when he did not move to follow, she quickened her pace. Just as she was about to enter the corridor that led to her bedroom, he spoke again.

"I must warn you, however, attempting escape through a window would not be wise. I have men stationed heavily outside this apartment. You will not make it far before you are apprehended and returned."

Her steps faltered, her head dropped, and the realization that she'd become a prisoner in her own home finally struck profoundly against her thoughts.

"I don't want to be here any longer. I don't want to stay with my husband and his ... whatever the hell this is."

He moved into the interior of the hall, the large size of his body blocking the light from the iron chandelier behind him, casting a shadow over hers. When she finally turned to look at him, she found that his features had softened, that pity weighed heavily on his heart.

"And I do not want to be the man who allowed Joseph's wife to leave him."

Chapter Nine

Arianna stripped off her clothes, dropping them along the floor in her path to the sunken shower in the large bathroom of her suite. Her eyes flicked to the open windows, seeking out any movement or signs of the presence of the men watching from outside. Moving to the window, she drew the curtains closed with such force, she almost ripped them from the rods.

Tears trailed down her cheeks, her stomach knotting over itself from the mixture of the lack of food and desperate grief. Stepping into the shower with heavy and weighted steps, each jolt against the floor resonated through her bones. She flicked the water on and stood back waiting for it to become warm.

"Tell me who owns you Arianna..."

A flash of black hair, the water running in rivulets down the face of a man she thought she'd known – the one that she still loved, despite what he'd done. Memories overtaking her from the day they'd first moved into the mansion, she stepped underneath the spray, watched as it streamed across her skin. Her muscles ached and were crippled by the emotional pain that had sprung within her, an avalanche from which she could not run or escape.

"You are the most beautiful sight I've ever seen – and to think that you are mine, always..."

Her lips parted, the water sliding along her lips and tongue when she responded to the phantom of her husband.

"And forever."

Resignation settled over her, but she wouldn't allow self-pity. She'd been foolish not to have noticed the signs of her husband's actions: the late nights, the fitful sleep, the obsessive mannerisms – but mostly, the way his moods bounced between anger and happiness – the former eventually smothering the latter.

But, she'd done nothing.

Shutting off the water, she stepped out, solemnly drying herself with a towel before moving into her large, walk-in closet and choosing a casual pair of pants and a t-shirt to wear. She knew Joseph preferred her to be dressed up, to appear as if she was the wealthiest woman around, but she could no longer play into the illusion of grandeur that had become his obsession – one that led him directly into the arms of a life rooted in crime.

After dressing, she laid down on the bed, pulling Joseph's pillow to her face and breathing his scent in deeply. She loved him, but the knowledge that she couldn't accept the life he'd chosen forced tears from her eyes once more.

Minutes passed quietly by while her mind wandered over the few years they'd lived in the mansion. Sleep crept up on her like a silent companion, but she was instantly awakened by the quick rap of knuckles against her bedroom door. She sat up, her eyes coming back into focus after being ripped back from a numb place.

She made two attempts to stand in her emotionally weakened state before giving up and answering, "Come in."

The green eyed man opened the door but did not move past the doorway. His expression carried a hint of concern, but it was fleeting in its duration. "Joseph has requested that I escort you to an event in the ballroom in an hour. He also requested that you dress up." His eyes traveled quickly over the pants and shirt she wore that were now wrinkled from her attempt at sleep.

She sighed. "And my *husband* couldn't have come to make the request himself? Have I become nothing more than a servant who is to answer only when he calls?" Bitter and aggrieved, her words were spoken with a harsh tone she'd not intended.

"Mrs. Carmichael..."

"My name is Arianna. If you are to be my jailor, you might as well use my name."

He smiled slightly, the dimples embedded in his cheeks once again showing through the shadow of stubble. "And mine is Connor, however, given that you are Joseph's wife, I'll prefer calling you by your married name."

A humorless laugh escaping her lips, she threw her hands up in defeat. "Of course…" Looking up at him, her expression carried more of a pleading quality than she'd wanted. "I've been delegated to an object that is owned, nothing more."

Connor's features remained blank, but the slight tension to his posture gave away just a bit of the thoughts that raced through his head. "He asked that you dress for a formal event. I'll be in the living room when you are ready to be escorted to the ballroom."

"And if I'm never ready? I'm not sure I want to know what my husband has planned for the evening…or that I want to see him." The last words trailed off quietly, an inner thought spoken aloud.

Nodding his head in her direction, Connor answered, "It's not your decision to make. I'll be in the living room."

After the light click of the lock, Arianna was left to dutifully follow Joseph's instructions.

. . .

Joseph sat in a large chair, positioned purposefully in the center of the small stage that stood in the front of the ballroom. To his side was a second chair intended for Arianna. He'd had tables arranged throughout the room, a touch of class required for an event worthy of his presence. The steel grey of his eyes moved over the room. Men shuffled in dressed in suit and ties, each one undoubtedly armed heavily. His eyes kept flicking over to the doors to the right wing. He was nervous to have his wife in attendance and he knew she'd object to the violence that was to take place, but he hoped that if she witnessed the control, the power, that he'd obtained over the network, the fear he'd seen darken her eyes that morning would dissipate.

While surveying the men as they filled the tables before him, he smiled slightly, pleased about the organization he'd created. These men weren't thugs. They weren't common criminals that ran the streets, desperately working to draw an income. No – these men were well-educated, influential characters who directed those less powerful, who sat back disguised and unnoticed while their underlings dirtied their hands with the work on the street. It was Joseph's diligence in his selection of the units' leaders that made The Estate so successful. Instead of multiple areas of crime fighting amongst each other in their efforts to gain ground, they worked together. It was a simple idea, one that not only increased the profit for Joseph, but also each unit involved. And now that the authorities were bought and paid for, there was no person to become inquisitive in their activities or muddy up the criminal dealings of those who were part of The Estate.

After the men had settled, Joseph heard the latch of the right wing doors; the groan of wood as the doors were pulled back announcing the arrival of Arianna. His eyes shot to the right and he watched as she entered the room, a sight to behold in a simple red gown that shimmered magnificently under the light cast by the large chandelier in the room. Her shoulders were held back, her chin set straight, and her stride carried a strength to it that Joseph had never before seen. His eyes narrowed from his attempt to discern why Arianna now appeared to march when she'd always before appeared to glide.

Connor entered behind her, a warrior as usual, dressed for combat rather than a formal affair. His boots fell heavily against the stone floor, the sound echoing off the walls when the room had fallen silent in response to the appearance of Joseph's wife.

She quickly climbed the stairs before moving across the stage to take her place at Joseph's side. Emory and Connor took their positions behind Joseph and Arianna and a hush fell across the room once more. Before speaking, Joseph looked to his wife seeking approval, but finding instead the expression of a woman scorned.

His eyes darkened and his head swiveled back to look over the audience.

"Gentlemen, thank you for coming this evening and on such short notice." His voice bellowed throughout the room, strong and dignified while addressing his men. "As you all know, I've worked very hard to create The Estate. It is an organization unlike any other, and I'm gratified that my selection of your groups has turned out favorably. We are a collective that benefits not only ourselves, but each other and we have all grown exponentially as a result."

He paused.

"That being said, I must now inform you about an incident that took place yesterday outside of my home; one that will not be tolerated and one that will require punishment as a result."

He heard a slight gasp from Arianna, before noticing out of his peripheral vision that she squirmed in her seat. Ignoring her obvious discomfort, he continued.

"Eleven men from one of the Estate's units believed they were more powerful than me – than *us* – as a collective. While walking yesterday, my wife..." He turned slightly to motion towards the woman who now had a look of absolute hatred written across her face. "...was attacked. I'll not detail the attacker's intent, because the only fact that is of importance is that it was attempted." Pausing again, he took a moment to look into the eyes of each man in the room. He observed their mannerisms, the slight furrow to their brow, or the movement of their body behind the table where they were seated. His search to determine if any others had been involved delivered no firm answers, but he was pleased to believe that each man in the room had found it a surprise to hear about the occurrence.

Standing suddenly, he walked towards the front of the stage and raised his hand to motion Emory to his side. Once Emory had crossed the short expanse of the stage and taken his place, Joseph stated, "Gentlemen – I wish to make it abundantly clear just how thorough and swift my reach is within this network. The man who attacked my wife was executed on sight, however, I am not stupid enough to believe he acted alone. Within less than twenty-four hours of the attack, I not only discovered the identities of his co-conspirators, but apprehended them as well." A sly smile slithered across his face when the room grew deathly quiet. Once Emory had made his way off the stage and was positioned by the doors to the west wing, Joseph looked away from the audience to nod towards Emory and indicate that it was time to open the doors.

Chapter Ten

Arianna straightened in her seat almost immediately when Joseph began speaking. Recognition slapping her across the face, she was reminded of another speech Joseph had given – years ago and in a different ballroom. It was the tone of his voice that chilled her so thoroughly; an apathetic severance from emotion and a lethal edge to his words that were spoken so eloquently, most would not detect the threat. It was that other side to her husband; the one that had remained hidden to her except for in those moments where he'd lost himself and hurt or scared her as a result.

Her eyes looked over the audience and followed the path of their attention and stares to the doors leading to Joseph's wing. Like a suffocating blanket, she held her breath, anticipation and dread assaulting her thoughts from not knowing what was hidden behind those large, wooden doors.

The loud clatter of the wrought iron handles sounded just before a slow creak reverberated through the room. As the doors parted and as light was allowed to filter in from the large hallway behind those doors, Arianna's eyes widened to see ten men, chained and hooded, being led single file into the ballroom. Three men, dressed in head to toe black, directed the line of chained men. When they'd reached the center of the ballroom, they were stopped and made to stand facing the stage. One by one, their hoods were removed revealing disfiguring injuries to their faces.

With his hands clasped tight behind his back and his feet held slightly apart, Joseph stood quietly above them. "Welcome, gentlemen. How nice of you to join us this evening."

Nothing. No emotion to his words at the sight of ten men who looked to have already been brutalized before being led into the room. Each man swayed on his feet, their eyes were swollen closed and blood and dirt was smeared across their exposed skin.

"Turn around."

Another chill brushed down Arianna's spine from the ice cold manner in which Joseph had given that instruction.

The men rotated slowly around until they faced the audience; murmurs and gratified grunts sounded when the members of that audience were faced with the brutality already executed against the men. Joseph didn't move and didn't speak while he waited for the audience to calm back to a point of attentive silence.

From the corner of her eye, Arianna noticed Connor move out from behind where she sat. He stepped towards the front of the stage, but stopped suddenly to bend down and whisper, "Close your eyes if you can."

Her eyes shot to his. He looked her over for only a second, before straightening and moving to descend the stairs and take a position behind the chained men.

Once Connor had taken his position, Joseph spoke again. "I want every man here tonight to look at the faces of ten men who attempted to attack not only me, but also the network that has made the rest of you more powerful for just being part of it. I was going to quietly do away with these men, however, I remembered that we are a collective and as such, their punishment should be decided upon by The Estate as a whole." Joseph took a few steps, his head turning as if he was eyeing each man that sat in the room.

"There are only two options – death or imprisonment. Therefore, in order to let your voice and your decision be known, I ask this: for those who want death, stand up, and for those who want imprisonment, remain seated."

Her gut churning painfully over itself, Arianna's muscles tensed when she saw how every audience member slowly rose from their seat. Hurriedly looking over their faces only terrified her more to notice how, like Joseph, these men displayed no expressions of horror or disgust at what Joseph was intending to do; but instead looked disinterested and bored as they voted for the death of the chained men. After each man had stood, Joseph stepped back from the front of the stage and sat down in his seat. Out of desperation to stop the impending slaughter, she reached over to him and placed her hand on his arm. He twisted to look in her direction and smiled. His voice kept low and with insanity alight in his eyes, he asked, "Do you see, Arianna – do you see what becomes of any man who threatens our home?"

Shock washed over her allowing tears to fall helplessly from her eyes. Not appearing to notice or care, Joseph looked back towards the audience. A smile curling the corners of his sculpted lips, he ordered, "Kill them."

"On your knees." Connor's voice rang out as he walked to the first chained man to the right and lifted his gun. Surprised by the blast, Arianna fell back when the first gunshot sounded. The noise was deafening and her horrified eyes were locked tight to the blood that burst from the man's head just before his body fell unceremoniously to the stone tiled floor below.

Close your eyes if you can...

He'd known what would be done to the men - he'd known what the members of the network would choose. It was a warning and when the second gunshot sounded, she listened to his advice. Clenching her eyes shut tightly against the horror being carried out before her, she raised her hands up to cover her ears in a futile attempt to block out the sound of murder and death.

One more shot - then another – and another; until ten shots had announced the death of ten men; slowly, methodically, and without reluctance or remorse.

Her head fell back against her chair just before she bent forward, folding in over herself in an effort to escape. Her mind swimming in adrenaline brought about by panic, she didn't dare open her eyes and she wouldn't remove her hands from her ears. Muffled sounds occurred around her; shuffling noises mingling with the highs and lows of male voices as the people in the room reacted to what had just occurred. Arianna felt alone, lost and exposed to the lunacy of her surroundings. When it felt like she would slide out of her chair despite how her muscles were locked across her bones, she felt hands grip her arms to pull her back up before her hands were forced from her ears so that someone could whisper to her.

"Arianna, open your eyes and look at me."

When she shook her head in refusal, Joseph demanded again, "Open your eyes, Arianna."

But still, she refused.

Forcefully, Joseph pulled her forward until he could wrap one arm around her back and one underneath her legs. After he'd lifted her from the chair, she felt him descend the stairs of the stage and quickly stride out of the ballroom. She heard the doors open and latch closed and then silence overtook her, except for the rhythmic pound of two sets of feet.

Joseph only slowed when they'd reached her suite and she assumed another man moved to open the doors once she heard the familiar creak of the hinges. Joseph entered the suite, immediately turning in the direction of their bedroom. Finally placing her down on the bed, his hand moved over her hair as if to soothe her.

When he spoke, she noticed how his voice and overall demeanor changed now that he was outside of view of the other members of his organization. "Arianna – speak to me, open yours eyes at least."

She obeyed, allowing the clear blue to peak out from beneath her lashes to look into the cool, yet concerned color of steel. Joseph stared at her for a few moments; the wrinkle to his brow and the sides of his eyes the only thing that betrayed his inner thoughts. She thought she saw a hint of compassion, of regret; but when he finally spoke, the only emotion that erupted from him was rage.

"How dare you? How dare you embarrass me like that in front of my men?! Why are you acting like this?" He sat back, only giving her enough room that she no longer felt the heat of his breath roll across her face. "Answer me!"

She cried out in fear at his raised voice and attempted to break free of his grasp. When she flinched at his tightened grip, he smiled again, but the black veins that dimmed the light grey of his eyes warned her that it wasn't humor or happiness he felt.

When he finally let go of her arm, he did so in a way that caused her to fall back on the bed, like nothing more than a doll thrown carelessly across the mattress. He stood up, took a few steps back, but never unlocked his eyes from her face.

"Are you going to answer me, Arianna, or do I need to force you?"

Her words were choked off by the sobs caught in her throat when she responded, "How did you expect me to act? You just had ten men killed in front of me. What did you think I would do?"

He snorted and an arrogant mask fell over his features, a sardonic look of concern and pity. "How about appreciating a husband who not only found, but ELIMINATED a threat against his wife. But instead, INSTEAD, you acted like a hysterical female!"

"That threat wouldn't have existed in the first place if it wasn't for you!"

Joseph seemed to flinch at the volume of her answer. His face twisted, multiple emotions rushing across the beauty of his features one after the other. When he stepped in her direction, she moved back, not sure how far her husband would go in his anger towards her. But he stopped short, his hand reaching up to tear through his hair, before he turned away from her entirely.

Looking past his shoulder, Arianna saw Connor in the doorway. As usual, he stood motionless; his green eyes jumping between her and Joseph, his entire body tensed as if he waited for something that would cause him to react.

In a calmer tone, Joseph said, "I need to return to the ballroom. When the meeting concludes, I'll return to deal with you." He didn't look back when he walked briskly from the room and disappeared into the shadow of the corridor. Arianna expected Connor to follow, but instead, he stepped inside the room and shut the door behind him once they could no longer hear the sound of Joseph's retreating footsteps.

Her eyes locked with his and she was surprised to find the compassion she'd hoped to find in her husband. He didn't move near her; his hand never leaving the handle of the door, he asked softly, "Are you okay?"

A humorless laugh escaped her - of course, she wasn't okay. She'd just been witness to slaughter and now she was locked in a room with the man who'd been the one to carry out the act.

Straightening out her dress, she calmed herself while keeping her eyes trained to the material. "Please leave." It was a quiet request, one that lacked strength or force; but it was one that caused Connor to push down on the handle of the door and let himself out into the hall.

Before completely exiting the room, he paused without turning to look at her. "I'm sorry you saw what you did. You should never have been there."

The soft click of metal and Arianna was left alone, a quivering heap sitting weakly in the center of her bed.

Chapter Eleven

It was hours before Joseph returned. Stumbling into the bedroom, he appeared disheveled, his clothes emitting a powerful stench of alcohol and smoke. His normally styled hair was messed up from where he'd run his hands through it and his normally grey eyes appeared black as coal.

Arianna remained on the bed, still dressed in the scarlet red gown she'd worn to the meeting in the ballroom. She'd fallen asleep after Connor left, her body giving out from the torrent of emotions that had assaulted her system over the last few days. She probably would not have woken upon Joseph's entry had he not fallen into the door before opening it.

He circled around the foot of the bed, his drunken gaze traveling lazily, hungrily over her body. "You're sleeping in your gowns now?"

Wiping the hair from her face, she looked down over her dress before quickly looking back up at her husband. "I...it's been a rough night. I didn't intend to fall asleep. I'll change." Pushing herself up from the bed, she moved to the side and stood up attempting to walk towards the closet. Within seconds, Joseph moved to her side of the bed and wrapped his hand tightly around her bicep.

"There's no need to change."

Arianna eyed Joseph wearily, understanding of his meaning slithering down her spine as each tired muscle in her body found the strength to spasm and lock. Her eyes closed slowly before opening again. "You can't be serious, Joseph. Not after last night ... or tonight."

However, he was serious, and when his hand reached up to find the hidden zipper at the back of the dress, Arianna attempted to shift away, only to have her arm squeezed tighter beneath his iron grip.

Dangerously low and slurred from the alcohol he'd consumed, his words agitated her, an abrasive sensation like sandpaper being scraped across her skin. "Will you fight me, deny me the duties owed by a wife to her husband?"

Looking up into his hooded eyes, Arianna sighed in resignation. She didn't want to fight him, didn't have the vigor to endure any additional abuses – but what choice was there? "And if I refuse?"

The corners of his lips curled up, a renewed heat rolling off his body against hers. Bringing his lips to her ear, he whispered, "I'd like that very much. Nothing turns me on more than conquest."

Moving so suddenly he hadn't had time to react, she freed herself of his grip and spun to face him. Anger brushed his features before his eyes followed her arm that reached behind her back to finish what he'd started.

Pulling the zipper of her dress open, she shrugged out of the material as it loosened over her shoulders and chest. It fell to her feet in waves of shimmering rubies and she stepped out of it, dressed in nothing more than the silken panties she'd worn underneath. The cool air meeting her skin induced a full body shiver, her skin prickling as the clear blue pools of her eyes met the jaded grey of Joseph's.

"I find it ironic." Her voice was cold, emotionless as she addressed the man she no longer knew. "You make a show of rescuing me from a man who intended to rape me, you destroy my world by admitting to what you've become, and then you force me to bear witness to a slaughter – and you do so in the name of protecting me, and in the name of showing me your *power*, your ability to bring punishment on those who attempted to hurt me."

Joseph wavered on his feet, but still lorded over her small stature, perfectly quiet as she spoke.

"And yet...here you stand, threatening to take what I will not give, committing the same crime against me."

He stared at her, his nostrils flaring out in anger before his hand moved quickly to her throat. His fingers tightly anchored against her skin, Joseph pushed her back towards the wall by the bed, pressed her firmly against the plaster with his eyes burning into hers and lifted her so that her toes barely brushed the ground beneath her. She didn't resist, didn't attempt to fight him off; her understanding of his deepening madness enough to keep her from angering him further. In that moment, as they stood nose to nose, passion filled grey eyes locked with the unfeeling blue, Arianna made a decision to escape, to endure whatever was necessary in order to find that one unwatched, unguarded second when she could run.

Joseph's eyes closed and his head fell back slightly, but when he pulled it back, when his eyes opened again, Arianna knew the man she loved was no longer there.

"You, Arianna, are an unappreciative, spoiled bitch of a wife." Tossing her to the floor, her head hit against the adjacent wall, a small cry escaping her lips from her surprise and pain. He stalked towards her, cruelty inlaid in the grin that touched his lips.

"I've given you luxury, I've given you a home, I've given you..." He stopped, a sick smile smearing across his features before he continued. "Ah yes, I forgot, you didn't want those things – it wasn't enough for the perfect princess I married. What you saw tonight, what I did for you, it was a display of power, of justice, of..."

"Of insanity, of a nightmare..." she softly added.

He reached down to lift her by her hair, only to backhand her so suddenly that she fell back to the floor once more. Warmth spread across her cheek where he'd struck her and she reached up to touch her lip, finding blood when she pulled it away.

Crawling away, she looked up at him and noticed how his eyes closed tight, giving him the appearance of a man pained. Opening them again, he said, "And of a woman in hysterics!" Reaching down and easily catching her, his hand gripped around her throat. She could barely breathe but tried to remain calm. She waited for the next strike, her breath ragged and her heart beating painfully against her chest.

Joseph appeared mad, a man attempting to control himself, but losing the battle, his violence leaking out against his wife. After several minutes of silence, he said, "Embarrass me again, Arianna, and I'll make sure you meet with a true nightmare. As for now, there is something you can give me, that you've *failed* to give me for far too long."

His hand gripped harder and his fingers tangled painfully deep within the silken strands of her hair. He lifted her again, but turned quickly to push her facedown against the bed.

Using her hair as reins, he controlled her and held her still for his abuse. The touch of his hand was callous and cruel as he ripped away the last bit of cloth that covered her. She felt him shift as he removed his pants, heard the belt hit against the tiled floors when it fell to his ankles. Finally positioning himself at her opening, he pulled her head up by her hair so that he could place his mouth to her ear. "You will give me a child, an heir, if I have to force this night after night until that happens, so be it. The level of pain is your decision. Fight me and this will be more agonizing than it needs to be."

Tears spilled from her eyes when his mouth and tongue moved across the skin of her neck, when his teeth bit sharply into the sensitive area at her shoulder. She cried out in pain, which only made him move one greedy hand quickly over her body and breasts while the other continued to pull at her hair. And even through the pain, she couldn't help but respond.

"You're sick! I'll never bring a child into this hellhole you're creating!"

He laughed, the sound disgusting and maniacal as he bent forward to say, "It's a shame that's not your choice any longer." Shoving himself inside, the sensitive skin between her thighs burned as tiny fissures were ripped open from his force. She cried out again when his girth filled her and her muscles ached from the sudden and uninvited intrusion. "Please Joseph, please stop!"

But instead of stopping, he seemed lost in his rage – pure madness stripping away all remaining sanity.

The hair at her scalp threatened to rip free as he held her still, raping her, freeing her of the last bit of love she'd had for him. When he'd roared out his release, and when his body collapsed over hers, he ripped her head to the side once more.

"I told you that you belong to me long ago, and regardless of whether you love me or hate me, that will never change. If you value your life, it's best you learn to accept it."

He pulled himself free allowing her to fall to the floor. She sobbed as he redressed, and as his footsteps grew faint when he left the room. Only when the door closed, did she allow herself to truly let go; crying, shaking, and drowning in the knowledge that he'd never let her leave.

Chapter Twelve

One deep, dark and resonating note filled the small space of the room. Arianna's eyes looked up at the music above the keys, squinted at the light and airy music contained on those pages, music that she could not play, could not bring herself to enjoy.

One finger, on one key, playing one note – over and over.

It was all she could manage.

Two weeks had passed, each night bringing more indignity, more rape. Her body felt bruised and battered, and her mind felt shredded and torn. She'd become a prisoner in her own home, an object for his use, his pleasure, a thing of so little value, that she'd been reduced to an empty shell devoid of emotion or light.

Connor stood at the door to the music room, his stance typical as he stood sentry over her. She grown accustomed to his presence, and oddly, she found comfort in his ever-watchful eyes. They'd spoken to each other only on rare occasions, and only when she'd responded to his statements or questions. However, as the weeks dragged on and as Joseph fell further into madness, dragging her along with him, Arianna couldn't speak, wouldn't voice anything openly or easily.

Up until this morning, she'd still been able to play, but the night before had been her worst. Joseph's tastes were becoming more vile, more depraved. He'd violated her in ways no man should be allowed, had torn at parts of her body, had chained her and gagged her, and he had done so while telling her he loved her still, and that in time, when she was fat with his child, she'd remember the promises made on their wedding night, their past desire for a child they could call their own. She knew he was sick; that his mind had twisted into something foreign and dark – a place from which there was little hope of return.

She'd grown numb to the abuse, to the added insult of his spoken words of love. Reaching a point where death was welcomed, she secretly hoped he would go too far, choking her free of her life, instead of just into unconsciousness.

Each morning that she woke up, she forced herself from bed and out into the living room. After the first week, she'd noticed how Connor's eyes would seek out new injuries, how they would hood over and darken when he'd found what he sought. He'd said nothing to her about it, hadn't made a move to approach her in the weeks that Joseph's abuse had occurred; so, when a deep voice spoke softly behind her while she sat playing that one key, she startled before turning to look into the eyes of emerald and jade that shimmered in light and were made brilliant against tan skinned and black hair.

"I'm sure you've heard this many times in your life, but you play beautifully."

She blinked in surprise, not having expected a compliment from the strong and silent guard in the room. Her eyes lowered to the floor, the intensity of his stare too much for her at that moment. She felt exposed, raw, and ashamed after the nights she'd spent with Joseph over the past few weeks. "Thanks, I guess." Turning back to the piano, she lifted her hands as if to finally play, but the only thing that fell on the ivory keys were the tears she could no longer contain.

The soft sound of boots against stone tile was the only warning before a large, strong hand fell tenderly on her shoulder. "Would you like to go somewhere else today, away from this building? It's been a while since you've seen the sun." His tone of voice was relaxed and compassionate, the baritone depth wrapping around her body like a warm blanket in winter. Arianna felt unsettled to feel comfort in his voice, his presence, but she accepted it nonetheless. Sometimes, when all a person is given is solitude and silence, having any human interaction is a blessing, regardless of its source.

Her mind traveled back to the last time she'd ventured outside, to the dense fog in the woods that had disguised the danger lurking nearby. Beside her stood another monster who had lumbered into the woods that morning, one she grown accustomed to since that fateful day.

"Do you trust me enough to take me out? What if I were to run, to never look back?" She knew she'd never make it if she tried, but that didn't stop the fantasy from playing endlessly in her mind.

"Come. Walking the grounds may do you some good." His hand still set on her shoulder, the warmth traveled through her skin, settling against the chill of her bones she was never able to escape.

"Will you get in trouble? Will *Joseph* approve?" She couldn't help the scorn in her voice as she said her husband's name. Twisting so that she could peer up at Connor through the thickness of her lashes, she noticed a slight twist to his mouth, and the faint indentation of the dimple on his cheek.

"Joseph's instructions to me were to keep you safe and away from his men and his wing. Other than that, where you travel is up to you, as long as you remain on the property."

A resigned sigh brushed across her lips and she nodded in agreement.

Reaching down, Connor took her hand to assist her from the bench and led her out of the music room towards the sunlight that awaited her outside.

The thick ground cover and leaves crushed and shifted under Arianna's feet as Connor walked her towards the path leading through the woods of the property. Her face turned up into sunlight, she closed her eyes to the glare but welcomed the warmth that brushed over her skin. Breathing in deeply, she shuddered to think how long it had been since she'd been outside and she was thankful to Connor for having made the suggestion.

As usual, he was silent when they walked, but he appeared determined in his lead. When they'd finally entered the shade of the canopies, Arianna cleared her throat before asking, "Is there anywhere in particular that we are going?"

He turned to her, gently taking her arm in his hand as he assisted her over some top roots of a large oak tree nearby. "Actually, yes. I had a lot of time to explore the land before Joseph asked that I watch over you. There are some hidden places dispersed over the property that are absolutely beautiful. When I wasn't on duty, I spent most of my time in some of them. There is one, however, which is the most beautiful of all. That's where I'm taking you."

Her interests peaked; she smiled shyly after he released her arm. "For as long as we've lived here, I've never had the chance to explore. Between the parties, and my music, and ... him ... the only time I ventured out into the woods was that day."

Connor nodded. "I'm sorry for what happened. I was lucky to be nearby, to hear when you cried out. I don't want to think what would have happened if I'd been farther away."

Laughing at his apology, Arianna considered the irony of his statement. "You only saved me from the pan to throw me into the fire."

His steps faltered at her words, his shoulders tensing and then relaxing at her implication. Without responding, he continued walking her deeper into the forest, stopping every so often to hold back a branch or assist her over difficult patches of top-seated roots that littered the path. The canopies of the trees left them obscured in shadows, but after an hour of walking, her eyes finally settled on an opening where light cascaded into the woodlands, bringing life and color to the trees and plants that it touched. Faintly, she could hear what sounded like rushing water and her eyebrows lifted as she attempted to peek around Connor's large form to see where he'd led her.

Finally breaking free of the shadow of the trees, Connor stepped to the side to give Arianna an unobstructed view of the place he'd wanted her to see. Her eyes widened as much as they could against the bright glare of the sun. Her jaw dropped from her shock at the beauty opened out before her. Taking hesitant steps, she moved towards the calm pool that was set off from the stream that ran over the property. The rocks glistened in multiple hues of gold, red and brown and the water running over them imitated sparkling diamonds as it traveled through the branches of sunlight that touched it.

The only sound she could hear was the water moving below her and the birdsong from the woods at her back. Looking out, she was awestruck by the colorful wildflowers that dotted the fields stretched out on the other side of the creek. It was beautiful, it was inspiring and it helped breath life back into her body.

Turning quickly, her eyes met with Connor's and her smile beamed out at him. "This place ... it's amazing, Connor. I had no idea it even existed on the property." She turned to look back out over the creek and field and was surprised when she felt the warmth of Connor's hand grasp hers. Looking up at him, she felt awkward, but she didn't pull away, curious as to why he'd made the effort to touch her.

"There's a natural cave nearby that I found, would you like to see it?" He smiled with a boyish charm and Arianna was shocked to discover a tender side to a man who killed without mercy. Nodding 'yes' to his offer, she allowed him to lead her around the creek and to a rock formation that jutted out from the wooded area nearby. As they walked, her eyes traveled over the landscape, marveling at how the scene looked as if it had been painted or a distant dream.

"Like I said, I spent a lot of time mapping out the property in order to decide how it would be best protected. There are several rock formations like this one, however this is the only cave I was able to find. I was concerned it could be a place for someone to hide, but it's at a good enough distance that I didn't worry about it. I'm not upset I took the time to find it though, I come here every once in a while when I need time to myself."

"You're with me all day, when have you had time to come out?" Her voice was strong for once, the nightmare that had become her life momentarily forgotten in response to her surroundings.

"At night when I'm excused from guarding you."

She knew he didn't intend to remind her, but his words brought that nightmare crashing right back in like a landslide. Her body trembled and her knees weakened at the reminder. Connor noticed her discomfort and wrapped an arm around her waist to steady her. She stopped short, the contact startling her even more than she'd already been.

Pulling his arm away, he apologized quickly. "I'm so sorry. I thought you looked like you could use a hand for support, I didn't intend..."

Arianna looked up at him, her eyes sparkling in the sun, two blue orbs swirling with multiple hues. "No please, it's fine. I just thought about having to go back and it upset me."

They walked into the interior of the cave and Arianna looked around at the glittering walls. "So, you come out here at night? Do you ever sleep?"

He smiled, the dimple on one cheek made more apparent by his expression. "Very little actually. I've even slept out here a night or two."

She chuckled half-heartedly. "I wish I could sleep out here. It has to be better than my room, more peaceful at least."

When his face fell, she changed the subject. "Do you live in the mansion?"

"I have a room in the west wing that Joseph gave me after I'd worked for him for a couple of months. He wanted more security on site twenty-four hours a day, so he arranged for a group of men to live in the mansion."

Sitting down on a rock, she looked up at him. "How many men live here?"

"On average, about thirty men live here, however, over the past few weeks that number has doubled. I guess Joseph feels more comfortable with the increased activity since you found out about the network."

Her curiosity got the better of her and since Connor was apparently talkative, she took advantage of his openness. "I'm surprised he was able to hide it from me. It seems strange that thirty men could come and go without my notice."

Nodding, Connor sat down next to her. "It's a large building and he kept the activity restricted to the west wing. Most people would not have noticed."

Leaning back, she could feel the heat of his body on her side. She welcomed the contact, however, happy to just be relaxing and having a normal conversation with someone other than herself. "What goes on over there? He always smells like alcohol and smoke when he returns for the evenings, he always appears manic and disheveled. Are there drugs? I assume he must have a hand in that if he's keeping company with criminals."

Seemingly hesitant to answer, Connor breathed out heavily. "I shouldn't be talking to you about this, Mrs. Carmichael. If Joseph found out..."

"Arianna. Please, just use my first name. Calling me by his surname feels like a punch to the stomach these days."

He looked over to her, sympathy evident in the clear green of his eyes. "If it's just us, I'll call you whatever you wish, however, in his presence or the presence of his men, I have to call you by a name that is proper. His obsession with you is upsetting. I understand a man loving his wife, but..."

Placing a hand on his, she silenced his thought. "I know – trust me, I know. But there's nothing that can be done about it. That is, unless you want to turn your head so that I can leave." Wriggling her brows at him, she caused him to smile brighter.

"It would cost me my life to do so."

A gasp escaped her before she could contain it. Even though she'd seen what her husband was capable of, it still surprised her to hear it. "No. Then that won't work. Maybe I'll just wait for him to pass out one night and sneak away when you're off duty."

"Please don't."

His response was so immediate it worried her. "Why not?"

He chewed at his bottom lip for a moment before answering. "When he visits you at night, he excuses me from the suite, but his personal guard, Emory, is always there with him. I'd hate for you to run into his guard, there is something off about him – something I don't trust." He quieted for a second, appearing to decide how he would say what he wanted to tell her. "I know your husband hurts you, I've seen the bruises and other marks, but he still loves you. If Emory were to get his hands on you, you wouldn't live to see the next morning."

Taking a moment to think about what he'd just divulged, Arianna looked out towards the mouth of the cave before speaking again. "Why is everyone so afraid of Joseph? He is one man, I don't understand how he came to be the most powerful, especially in a group of men who seem to lack any sense of morality."

"Your husband is a very intelligent man. He keeps the network working together instead of against each other. Each man has become wealthier as a result. In a group such as that, money speaks. Joseph has also found a way to keep the authorities from investigating their crimes. That alone is enough for each man to defend the organization and to protect Joseph if it came to it. Fighting him would mean fighting hundreds of men. It's not worth the risk."

Her head swam with the information Connor gave her. She'd known that Joseph's *business* was large, but she'd never imagined the true extent of his reach. "The authorities?" A humorless laugh escaped her. "So even if I were to escape…"

"You'd be found and returned to your husband."

A golden curtain of hair tumbled forward as she brought her face to her hands. Finally lifting her face, she stood up and walked out into the sunlight. She allowed the heat to dry the tears that fell along her cheeks and could feel Connor when he walked up behind her. He stood so close, his body heat rolled over her back. After a few moments, she asked, "How did you end up a killer?"

At first she thought he wouldn't answer, but then she heard a resigned sigh just before he said, "I was abandoned when I was young and I grew up on the streets. It was a bad area – kill or be killed. I'm good at what I do and when I was found by a group of men, they employed and educated me."

Turning to him, her eyes met with the broad expanse of his chest. Musk and a touch of spice, his scent enveloped her before she could step back to look up into his face. "Do you agree with what my husband is doing to me? Is it something you're okay with?"

"No." Hard, assured, and instantaneous, his response surprised her.

"Then why do you work for him?"

His lips twitched and he appeared uncomfortable with how he should answer. "I accepted the job before I knew what Joseph would become. When I started here, he wasn't doing the things he does now. I blame Emory's influence for that. I stay now because I don't have any choice but to stay."

"Why don't you have a choice?"

"Because I won't leave you here alone."

Taking a few steps back, her brow furrowed as she tried to understand what he was saying. "You still have a choice."

His eyes left hers and he looked out over the water behind her. She continued staring into the endless green, patiently waiting for his response.

His eyes finally meeting hers once more, he said, "I won't leave you here to die and taking you from here would only end in death for us both. In time, that might change, and I'll stick around just in case the opportunity presents itself; but for now, we have to stay." He paused for a moment, his eyes moving back to glance at the water. Softly, he added, "I'm sorry, Arianna, but there is no choice."

Chapter Thirteen

"Tell me you love me, Arianna. Remind me how you can't live without me!" The hard slap of knuckles against her cheek and she fell against a wall in the corner of the room.

Crouched down in her corner, she attempted to avoid Joseph's hand when he reached out for her again. It was futile to fight and she knew that; but even though her mind told her to endure, her instincts told her to fight. His fingers tangled into her hair and the cold stone tile rubbed against her skin when he dragged her across the floor. When they reached the bed, he used his other hand to grasp the shackles he'd attached to the bed months ago.

But, it wasn't every night.

Over the time that he'd practiced his abusive ritual against her, there were nights when he didn't show and she was left in a restless sleep, never knowing if she would hear the click of the lock or the creak of the door as he entered.

She was tired. Bags hung heavily beneath her eyes and she'd lost weight from lack of eating. It took more and more makeup each time Joseph held a party at their home; each time demanding she present herself as nothing more than his loving wife. The party attendees had changed over time. What had once been mutual friends soon became the men of his network and the women they brought with them. Arianna spent most of those nights blending into shadow, not interested in conversing with the evil Joseph kept for company.

The soft click of metal and Arianna felt the pinch of a shackle as it closed around her ankle. Falling heavily on the mattress, she pulled her arms under her and braced herself for what she knew was to come.

. . .

The cold water rushed across her bare feet; a stream of ice that helped soothe the broken skin at her ankles and contrasted sharply against the heat of the sun that warmed her head and back.

"Your ankles look really bad today. I'm not sure I can stay quiet about this much longer." Connor sat on the grass near the stream's edge, mindlessly grabbing pebbles and tossing them into the water.

She looked over at him, a sympathetic smile gracing her features. "You'd only be killed for saying anything. It's been months and he appears to be getting worse. But at least his visits have become less frequent. And when he does show up, sometimes he loses the ability to, well...to finish. He's passed out a couple of times." A sad laugh escaping her, she added, "I've thought about bashing his fucking head in when that happens, but then I remember Emory is in the living room, and I'd rather not be left to whatever he would do if I killed Joseph."

"Maybe I should just kill Emory." Bitterness dripped from Connor's words.

"So that Joseph can replace him with another? I've heard several voices in the living room lately. I think he's added to his personal security. Maybe he's pissed off someone as crazy as him and they'll take care of the problem."

Connor looked out over the water. "I could kill him, it would end things for you."

Arianna flicked her toes over a small rock in the water. "You'd die."

An arrogant grin spread over his face. "They'd have to catch me first."

Turning towards him, she tried to smile, but it was a sad attempt at best. "It's not worth the risk. How many men does he have living over there now?"

"Hundreds."

She nodded. "Like I said, it's not worth the risk. Maybe he'll grow tired of me; put me out of my misery."

"I wouldn't waste much hope on that - he's too focused on getting you pregnant. I don't understand it. Why would he want a child?"

Turning her gaze back to the babbling creek, she sighed. "He's wanted one since we got married. He still believes he loves me; he tells me so when he does the things he does. I wonder sometimes if he believes a child would make me love him again. He's a sick man...it's such a shame because he was brilliant when we were first married." Laughing, she added, "Although, he never did have a lick of common sense."

Connor chuckled at her comment. "That's usually the way it works." He grew thoughtful for a moment. "It's getting worse in his wing. Drugs, parties, whores..."

Arianna closed her eyes. She'd suspected the things Connor was telling her, but hearing it confirmed only made it worse. Stepping carefully over the wet stones, she made her way over to where Connor sat. Sitting beside him, she pulled her knees to her chest, wrapping her arms around her legs before leaning into his side. They'd become friends over the months and she'd grown to trust in him as a friend and confidant. She knew he was being driven crazy in his knowledge of what happened to her some nights, but she'd never permit him to do anything about it. She cared too much about him to let him waste his life in an attack against Joseph.

His arm went around her, pulling her closer against his strong chest. They sat quietly, their eyes looking over the stream and field they walked to almost every day. It was a respite from the prison, a hidden dream within the nightmare.

"At least we have this place, huh? Somewhere we can escape, if only for a few hours." Her voice was wistful and soft.

Laying his head against hers, Connor hugged her closer. She felt so small next to him, so soft in comparison to the strength of his chest, his shoulders and his arms. Lost in his scent and the feel of him, she startled when he spoke again.

"I'll steal you from him someday."

She felt him kiss her softly on the top of her head, his hand moving to smooth down her back. She knew she should stop him, pull away and put distance between them, but she yearned for a tender touch after so many months of abuse.

"I know you'll take me away from here when you can. Hopefully, I won't be completely broken when that occurs."

. . .

She looked over his body, as it lay motionless on her mattress. The sheets that were twisted around his legs and his back moved slowly up and down while he slept. It had been a year and a half, his visits had become less frequent, but

128

every now and then she was met with the monster he'd become. Until tonight, it had been several months since she'd seen him, and she was taken by surprise when he'd entered the room staggering over his own feet before laying down next to her and falling asleep. She'd woken when he entered, but pretended that she hadn't. She was surprised he'd passed out beside her, the typical pungent odor of alcohol permeating his hair, skin and clothes. She could hear Emory and a group of men in the living room, laughing and carrying on. And her bedroom was the last place she wanted to be.

Slipping into her closet, she dressed herself in head to toe black. It was a new moon that night and there were very few lights left on around the mansion. Quietly, she unlatched the window, opening it slowly before crawling outside. She prayed Joseph wouldn't wake up while she was gone, but she had grown braver in the months since he'd started his abuse. Once she was fully outside, she looked back in and was gratified to hear him still breathing deeply on the bed.

Looking out over the shadowed yard, she crept low to the ground until she'd reached the cover of the woods. Moving quickly, she stumbled a few times over top roots, but she knew the path so well, that she was able to find her way to the stream where she spent her days. Her breath came easily once she heard the soft gurgle of rushing water and she moved to sit down on the rocks that lined the edge of the creek. Tears falling from her eyes, she feared Joseph would wake while she was gone, but she couldn't bring herself to go back to the room where she knew he lay sleeping. When her eyes finally dried, she wiped away the remnants from her cheeks and turned her face up into the infinite, star-filled sky. Silently, she prayed that something would change; that maybe, she could awaken from whatever twisted reality her life had become and discover that it all had been a dream.

The slight crunch of pebbles under a boot caused her to jump. "What are you doing out here, Arianna? If you're caught..."

"I don't care." Her words were unintentionally spiteful and curt. "I don't care about anything anymore, Connor. What's the worst he can do? Beat me?" She paused, a humorless chortle escaping her before she added, "He does that already. In fact, in the last few months, it seems like that's all he does."

Connor didn't move to approach her and his presence at her back felt familiar, like when he'd first been assigned to her guard. "Shit." His murmured swear surprised her, she'd never heard or seen him behave with anything but absolute control over his emotions and actions. "At least, come in the cave with me."

"Why? If they notice I'm gone, that's all it will take for him to punish me. It won't matter where I'm found."

Finally, after a few awkward minutes, Connor sat down beside her. "How did you get out?

Emory had at least five men with him. More may have arrived after I left."

"A window. Joseph passed out almost immediately when he arrived. I left him sleeping in the room. I just wanted to be out of there, away from him, from that place. Because, here, I can pretend like it isn't happening, that I didn't make the mistake of marrying a monster. I can pretend to be living a different life..." Tears again, but they weren't accompanied by the sobs of a distraught person. Those tears had disappeared months ago and were replaced with ones filled with frustration and anger.

Placing his arm around her shoulder, Connor used his other hand to pull her chin around so that she faced him. His thumb brushed over her cheek to wipe away a tear when he said, "I wish there was a way to get you out of this. I've been trying to come up with something, but every action I could take would lead to more problems. If I kill him, would you be able to escape his men? If I help you escape, where would you go? I'm angry with myself for not having helped you leave when it first started, maybe then, there would have been a chance. But, over time, he's grown stronger, pulled more people to his side. He's erected walls around you, ones that I'm not sure even I could help you get around."

Considering his words, Arianna didn't immediately respond. Finally finding words adequate to convey her thoughts, she said, "Years ago, I would have imagined it impossible for my husband to become what he's become; I would have fought tooth and nail with any person who even suggested it could be possible. But, looking back over the years, there were signs...symptoms. And I think that's what scares me the most. His madness wasn't always there, it was gradual, a slow decay that snuck up on me, that left me unsuspecting so that I could not act against it. So, does that make me blind or stupid?"

His hand squeezed her shoulder and she leaned into him in response. His voice soothed her, even though his words were utterly frightening in their truth. "There's a fine line between many things; love and hate, light and dark, brilliance and madness. Much like when the sun rises, the light it gives still touches on the darkness that it destroys. And it's in that place, the moment between sunrise and day and sunset and night, that is the scariest of all, because they are so closely linked that one cannot always be distinguished from the other. From what you've told me, it seems that Joseph has stood on that precipice for a long time. But I've noticed that people who finally succumb to the dark - to evil - it's not a dramatic shift, it happens slowly and without warning. However, in order for it to happen, they had to have been straddling that line and therefore, the madness had been a small part of him since the beginning because he was at a place where the two halves touch. You can't blame yourself for not seeing it. You loved him, you wanted to believe the illusion he created, but in that time, he fell too far, allowing you to finally recognize what he may have been all along."

Chuckling, she answered, "Well, that was confusing and insightful all at the same time." She nudged his chest with her shoulder before adding, "But I understand what you are saying." In a softer tone, she admitted, "Although I fear what he's already become, if you are correct in what you said, I'm even more afraid of how much farther he could fall."

Chapter Fourteen

Three months passed. In that time, Joseph's visits to Arianna grew more infrequent and there had been full weeks when he'd not shown up in her wing. But on the nights when he did appear, she'd learn to temper his violence by submitting without complaint or a fight, to lie numbly beneath him until he finished or passed out. He was still intent on a child, and she couldn't fathom how, in all this time it hadn't occurred.

Due to what appeared to be a waning obsession with her, she wondered if he'd grown tired of her, and she spent many hours thinking that, maybe, he'd have her killed, just to be done with her. The thought horrified her - not because she feared for her own life, but rather, she feared for Connor's. She knew that if the attempt was made, or if they succeeded, he would die fighting for her.

Her friendship with Connor had grown far too close and it was becoming apparent that they both looked to each other for more than just a platonic bond. However, they never overstepped a line in their friendship, until one fateful day...

"You should be careful jumping around on those rocks like that. The water is freezing and if you slip…"

"You're not worried about me falling in because it'll be cold for me…you just don't want have to jump in to save me." Her head fell back allowing the sun to bathe her skin in its warmth.

Looking out at a beauty dressed in white, Connor chuckled. "Well, yeah, there is that. But seriously, please come back over to the shore." He looked up at the sky. The sun shown brilliantly down on the field, but its light was threatened by the blackened clouds that also hung menacingly in the air. "It looks like it could rain at any time, I'd hate for you to be caught out there if the clouds suddenly released."

She peeked up at him, the blue of her eyes glinted beautifully within the sunlight and her golden hair cascaded around her shoulders, moving like spun silk when she turned her head. "If it's that important to you, fine." Jumping from one rock to another she returned to shore, finally taking a seat at his side.

"I've missed coming out here. I'm glad the winter has finally passed. Being stuck in that place… I don't know what I would have done all these months if it wasn't for my music, or you."

Quickly glancing in her direction, he smiled. "At least it's not as bad as it was before. He's been preoccupied over the past several weeks. I'd be lying to say it hasn't been a relief."

135

"That's true, but, for the life of me, I can't understand why he keeps me. I know he still believes he loves me, and I wonder if on those nights that he does return, if maybe the man he'd been before was closer to the surface than the one he's become. It's like there are two people inside him, battling over control, over sovereignty of the body they inhabit."

A raindrop touched her nose and she looked up instantly. Before they could move to react, the sky opened and rain fell so heavily, so suddenly, they could barely see five feet in front of them.

"Fuck!" Connor cursed before grabbing her hand and pulling her towards the cave. Once inside, Arianna laughed delightedly, finding humor in something as simple as being caught in the rain. Wringing out her hair, she looked down at her clothes and noticed that the light, airy material had glued itself to her skin, hiding nothing of her form. She was immediately embarrassed and looked up to find the green of Connor's eyes locked to her body, the heat of his stare absolute in its intensity.

Neither spoke, and, like magnets, they moved towards each other, hopelessly drawn together without thought or hesitation; but when their faces were inches apart, Connor leaned down and softly brushed his mouth against hers. She knew she should push him away, that she should turn away and prevent a mistake that would surely happen in this moment. But she couldn't and when the heat of his lips pressed deliciously against her, she parted her lips to allow him deeper. His tongue swept out, filling her mouth with his scent, his taste. Her knees weakened beneath her and his hand came around to brush across her back and hold her steady while his other traveled up the side of her torso, barely brushing across the side of her breast.

Just as suddenly as they'd begun, she forced herself to pull away. Her body trembled and her mind swam with the intensity of an emotion she'd not felt for a long time.

She looked up into Connor's face and saw that his brow furrowed and his eyes clenched tightly together. She could tell by his expression that he fought the same internal battle against his sudden desire. Bringing her hands up to the hard planes of his chest, she pushed away from him; fear coating her stomach at what would occur if she allowed what was developing between them to happen.

They stood motionless, facing each other silently while their chests heaved and their hearts pounded loudly within their bodies. The tension between them was suffocating and Arianna's skin tingled in anticipation of a touch she didn't want to crave as much as she did.

"Arianna – I'm sorry, I shouldn't have…"

She put her hand up to silence him. "We can't." Defeated, she breathed out, sadness saturating every cell of her body.

"I know." His expression looked pain as he stared down at her. The only sound that could be heard was the pounding of rain outside of the cave and every few minutes thunder rolled along the skies just before lightening provided flash illumination to his features. Arianna's eyes looked over his body, noticing how his wet shirt clung to every muscle that rippled along his chest and arms. She longed to reach out and remove the shirt, to run her hands along what she imagined would be smooth skin stretched taut across his body. Losing her control, losing sight of the nightmare in which she lived, she stepped towards him. She didn't care, couldn't fight, and eventually found herself so close to him, she had to crane her neck just to peer up into the beauty of his face.

"I'm a married woman, Connor..."

"The man you married no longer exists." It was a plea, one she could hear desperation and longing dripping from as it was spoken.

Her eyes searched his, the words he'd just spoken ringing truthfully in her ears. He was correct, but incorrect at the same time. The Joseph she'd met and married, no longer existed, he was correct about that; however, the monster that replaced him, the one who kept a hold on her despite whether he truly loved her or not, that Joseph was more terrifying, more of a threat than the person he'd formally been.

Connor stepped away from her, his eyes traveling over her face, deep longing lighting his eyes despite the shadows that covered them in the cave where he stood. His voice was quiet, reserved, when he spoke again. "Just tell me this, Arianna, tell me I'm not crazy for thinking that if circumstances were different, if fate had been more kind in the way that it brought us together, that there could have been something...something good..."

Her heart skipped as she listened to him babble on. He appeared lost to what he was trying to say, as if speaking the words aloud made them more impossible to be true than they had when they'd been locked within his mind.

"...I never had much of anything growing up, just bad luck and people who could care less about me. It wasn't until I started fighting that I held any value for someone. And a woman like you, one who exudes beauty in everything she does – the way you walk, your music, the way your eyes sparkle when you laugh – you were never the type I had any chance of finding. I know that if hell exists on Earth, we are trapped within it, but I'm amazed every day that somehow, within these walls that close in around us, and under the roof of a madman, you still find the ability to exude that beauty, a light that is strong enough to pierce the ever encroaching darkness, one that banishes the hollow and empty feelings of loss that come with living inside of a waking nightmare."

Trembling, she brought her hand to his cheek. Her eyes glistened with unshed tears and her mind struggled to wrap itself around what he was attempting to say. Her instincts screamed for her to resist his temptation, yet her heart and body wanted nothing more than to give in to the moment, despite what could happen as a result.

She didn't respond, having lost the ability to speak around the lump that settled fully in her throat from the emotions she struggled desperately to swallow. Finally, after losing herself to the battle she fought with herself, she answered, "I want to thank you, for everything you've done or try to do for me. I know you risk yourself daily bringing me down here, helping me escape if only for a few hours a day..."

Resting a single finger against her lips, he silenced her. A smile touched his lips and dimples that gave him a look of boyish innocence peeked out beneath the stubble on his cheeks. "Don't thank me. I'm a selfish man. When I bring you out here, it's partly for you – but mostly, it's just an opportunity for me to get you alone, to pretend that our lives are different, that you'd married me instead of a man not worthy of even your passing glance."

Without another word, he bent down, wrapping his large hand around her head and pulling her into a kiss that was so full of emotion, her knees finally gave out. He caught her around her back, deepening the kiss while laying her down on the ground of the cave. She didn't resist, didn't put up one bit of a fight against him. Violently, her body responded to his touch, heat flaring along her skin where his fingers trailed her body. Rain fell in curtains outside the mouth of the cave, as if nature itself wanted them to have this one beautiful moment without fear of being caught. Thunder continued to vibrate across the skies, and lightening illuminated the cave, casting erotic shadows on Connor's large form when he pushed himself up to remove the sodden shirt that covered his body. Her eyes widening, she watched the muscles of his shoulders and chest move beneath his tanned skin, highlighting the virility of the man undressing before her. Electric sparks tingling across her skin, her body warmed, readied itself for whatever he planned to do to her. It was an intoxicating feeling, an illicit affair that she'd never dreamed of before, but didn't think she could live without from that moment forward.

His hands grasped the hem of her skirt at her hips, pulling away the material, his heated gaze traveling along her skin that was slowly revealed to him. She sat up and allowed him to remove her shirt, and when her breasts were freed, the warmth of his hands instantly grasped around their weight, a moan escaping her throat at the way his touch sent waves of pleasure rolling through her body. When his mouth found the pebbled tip of her breast, his tongue flicked out as he took it deeper into his mouth, suckling softly and igniting sparks within her core. She became lost to his movements, the feel of his hands against her skin, the heat of his tongue moving across her body. Her back arched up, her head, hips and feet, the only parts of her left touching the floor where she laid helpless to his desire – his need.

Keeping his hands firmly gripped over her breasts, his fingers pinching and pulling at the hardened peaks, his mouth traveled up her body, licking along the delicate skin of her shoulder and neck, until settling on the sensitive lobe of her ear. His breath rolled along her skin when he said, "You are so fucking beautiful, I want to take you agonizingly slow, to bathe every inch of your body in my touch, my kiss."

She turned her head to face him, but her eyes closed when his mouth fell on hers, the force of his kiss causing her to feel drunk, yet alive. Her hands smoothed up the hard contours of his back until her fingers found and tangled themselves within the silken strands of his hair. Tugging slightly, she felt a growl that emanated from the depths of his chest, the vibration along her skin evoking a natural instinct to be dominated and overtaken by such a feral man. Breaking the kiss, his hands and mouth worked their way down her body, her head falling back as his lips traveled along her stomach. Finally, he found the band of her panties and pulled them down and along her legs, until she was freed completely of her clothes.

He pushed himself up, his hands resting gently on her thighs, spreading her legs before him and the green of his eyes blazed with a fire she'd never before seen. He took a moment staring down at her, an unreadable expression across his face, and the corners of his lips tilting up as he said, "I could sit here and look at you forever and it would never be enough." She trembled beneath his stare, unable to respond, her ability to speak, much less think, lost to the fervor of her body, to her reaction of his scent that lay completely across her skin.

Her legs fell easily out to her sides; every inch of her exposed to the intensity of his stare. His head dropped and his lips found the inside of her thigh, licking and nipping at her skin, traveling towards the place where she desperately needed him to be. A clandestine moment shrouded in the protective blanket of rain, her heart raced, blood pumping through her veins, a rush of hormones leaving her drunk and wasted to the workings of her body. When he lips finally met the sensitized flesh between her thighs and when his tongue flicked out to brush across the bundle of nerves that sat atop, her entire body quaked, bucking up against him, nature taking control over her ability to think clearly or care about the consequence of what they'd started.

His fingers gripped tightly to her thighs, holding her legs so wide apart that the tendons burned from the strain. Her hips rolled from the feel of his mouth on her skin, but when one hand found its way up, when one finger pressed at the opening to her body only to slowly push its way inside, her mouth opened in a silent cry of pleasure and pain, of desire and unbridled lust.

A long forgotten energy built within her, swirling deep inside her core, threatening to tear her apart if not released. Her muscles locked over her bones and her breath caught in her lungs. One finger became two and eventually they found their way to a spot inside her that drove her over an sensual edge so steep, stars burst beneath the lids of her clenched eyes. She lost control of herself, her awareness of their surroundings, and the world to which they would return completely forgotten, drowned beneath the way he made her feel, the passion he forced through her body with stunning and soul-consuming violence.

Her back arched, pushing the peaks of her breast up into the chilled air of the cave, but slowly, she regained her senses, electric jolts still erupting sporadically through her body, the tremble in her legs growing rapidly as her body let go of the tension, the anger and the pain that had been built over the last year she'd lived at the mansion.

Opening her eyes, she peeked up to find Connor sitting in absolute awe of the woman he watched intently, the curl to his lips deepening the dimples on his cheeks until she couldn't help but smile back up at him, small bits of laughter escaping her on her exhalation of breath.

She watched his hands move down to unbuckle his pants, every bit of him exposed as he pushed the material down, moving slowly to remove it from around his ankles and feet. His body was rock solid, hard in every place a man should be, and the tan to his skin spread even to those places the sun would not have touched. He was perfection, an Adonis looming over her, the physique of a warrior made even more beautiful when the light kiss of lightening reflected off his skin. He exuded carnal power, raw and unrestrained and Arianna's breath caught at the sight of him.

His hands gripped her hips, the fingers digging into the flesh as he lifted her to where he could position himself at her core. Their eyes locked and she noticed she'd stopped breathing in anticipation for his intrusion. He smiled, light sparkling within the emerald green of his eyes and in one fluid motion, he pushed himself inside, exquisitely filling her and stirring to life the volcano of need that'd almost reduced to her to ash only a few minutes before. Her mouth fell open, but the passionate cry that sounded was swallowed when his weight fell over her and his lips sealed over hers taking her breath, her cries, and his name as it rolled off her tongue.

Moving within her with a rhythm that eventually drove him deeper inside, he broke the kiss, and pushed up to look down at the small woman beneath him. He sped up, pushing them both hastily to a point where words could not be formed in their minds or on their tongues. Her hands ran along his back, her fingers smoothing over the skin covered with a sheen of sweat from the heat being poured from his body. It was carnal pleasure, completely overwhelming them both until finally, they found their release together. His lips parted and a feral growl escaped his chest, his throat while she screamed out, pushing a ball of energy from within her, an orgasm too vivid and powerful to contain. Finally, he lay down beside her, taking her into his arms and delivering to her the peace that had been stolen so many months before.

Chapter Fifteen

"I don't understand why you bother keeping her around. It's obvious she's unable to give you what you want...an heir. Why not just get rid of her and use one of the other women within the network who would happily give you what you need?" Emory sat back against the leather couch in Joseph's office. His fingers brought up to his face, he looked over his nails while attempting to convince Joseph to take the final step to setting himself free of a woman who'd caused nothing but problems since the network was built. "She poisons you, Joseph. You are too busy and important to be concerning yourself with something that has become useless - an anchor to a life you no longer live."

Rage bloomed within Joseph's chest at Emory's words and the nonchalant tone in which he spoke them. Bending forward he picked up a straw from the surface of his desk, placing it to his nose before inhaling the sweet escape of the drug he had lined up before him.

His head swam, his thoughts flickered out for a split second while the drug crept into his blood stream and followed a numbing path along his veins. His habit had started slowly, a way to temper the rage he felt at his failing marriage, the humiliation he daily suffered not being able to produce a child with Arianna. It was a nagging thought at first, but his obsession grew quickly, but not so much with the desire for a child as it was with his need to prove his own virility. It was an accomplishment not achieved and a failure he could not accept.

When Joseph didn't respond, Emory stop examining his hands and looked up with eyes so dark, the brown appeared black and lifeless. "I don't even know why you want a child so badly. Who will care for the vile thing? Certainly, not you."

"Arianna will care for it. She would be its mother – and it will be her, not some two bit whore that births him. Do you really think I'd muddy up the gene pool by impregnating some dumb bitch?"

The angry tone to Joseph's words caused Emory to straighten where he sat. Joseph eyed his guard intently before continuing. "Have you ever wanted immortality? I do - because I know that at some point, I'll no longer exist. Yet, I can beat even death itself by leaving behind a genetic link, something that can take over, to be a reminder of having existed at all." He paused, a wicked smile touching the sides of his lips. "Besides, who would manage The Estate when I die? Do you think I'd trust it to just anyone? It's as much a child to me as anything Arianna can push out of her body. If I have a son, I can raise him to be stronger than me, smarter, deadlier.

My network will never fall apart, even years after I'm still able to run it."

After lowering his head to inhale another line, Joseph sat back and allowed his head to fall to the side, his eyes watching the heavy rain that fell outside his window. The woods were all but obscured by the violence of the storm. Every so often lighting would crack the sky before the answering thunder would roll so loudly, it shook the windows and walls of the mansion.

Turning his head back to Emory, he reached out to cut more lines of the drug that was slowly eating away at his sanity. "Honestly, I could care less about the bitch. Ever since I told her about what I'd built, the successes I'd gained, all she fucking wanted was to leave. It'll be fitting to force her through a pregnancy, to show her that, without doubt, she belongs to me, regardless of whether she likes it or not."

Emory smiled, playing the devil's advocate, he asked, "Are you not concerned about how much time she spends with Connor? Their daily walks out into the woods? How sure are you that he's not working towards the same goal as you?"

Joseph stopped chopping and slowly placed the razor blade aside before looking up at his guard. "Do not mistake me for a fool, Emory. Connor is not that stupid...and neither am I. I have men watching them constantly. All that's been reported to me is that Connor guards her as he should, never touching her or barely even talking to her." He paused, a sick smile creeping along his features. "Not that Arianna would have anything to do with a man like him anyway. He basically ensured that they day he beheaded a man in front of her." He sat up and placed his elbows on the desk. "I know my wife, Emory. She's a prude, she's a tease; but she's not a whore. I have little concern about that."

. . .

Two weeks passed since Arianna and Connor had been in the cave and Arianna stood in her bedroom looking at a calendar, counting the days on her fingers that she was late.

"No." One word, whispered so low that only she could hear it. She moved away from the wall, paced the floor in front of her bed, fighting tears from falling down her face. She'd hoped it wouldn't be possible, but the signs, the sickness, told her that not only was it possible, it had occurred. Growing dizzy from the rush of emotions combined with the constant movement of her body across the floor, she finally sat on her bed, holding her head between her hands to keep from throwing up.

She'd woken up that morning feeling fine. Joseph hadn't shown up for over three days and she'd gotten out of bed and walked into the bathroom to take a shower and brush her teeth. The shower was uneventful but when she leaned over the sink and scrubbed at her teeth, her gag reflex kicked in and she found herself quickly bent over the toilet throwing up whatever bit of dinner still remained in her stomach from the night before. Forcing herself back on her feet after she'd spent several minutes dry heaving, she moved into the bedroom closet and put on a simple dress that wouldn't press on her sensitive stomach.

Now sitting, glancing up at the clock on the wall, she knew Connor waited in the living room to escort her to breakfast and then the music room. It was their daily routine on the mornings following Joseph's absence. Connor had started sleeping in the guest room on those nights, a secondary guard sent down by Joseph always stationed in front of the front doors to the suite.

She couldn't go out there and face him, face anybody without fear that she'd immediately break down, crushed by the knowledge that she would bring a child into the nightmare that had become her life.

Lying back on the bed, she stared up at the small iron chandelier that hung from the ceiling, her legs hung over the sides, her foot kicking back and forth. She heard the slide of metal against the tile floor when her toe brushed up against the shackle that Joseph kept attached to the foot of the bed. Instantly, she pulled her legs up, sitting up to wrap her arms around her knees, tears streaming down her face when she allowed herself to look down at the floor, her eyes finding the bits of the chain links that she'd accidentally dragged into view.

A soft knock at the door and she used her toe to quickly kick the chain back under the bed, the sound of metal against stone causing her stomach to turn and a chill to run up her spine. The door clicked open and Connor peeked into the room, his eyebrows raised in question at her obvious distress.

"What's wrong?" He pushed into the room, quickly crossing the floor to kneel down at the foot of the bed.

Turning her head away, she closed her eyes, avoiding the depth of the jade green eyes that stared up at her. She didn't want to tell him, didn't want to see the painful expression that was sure to cross his face. She felt his hand grab hers just before he stood up to take a seat next to her on the mattress. The bed sinking beneath her from his weight, she continued in her refusal to look at him when she said, "Get off the bed, Connor. I wouldn't be surprised if he had cameras in this room, or the entire house for that matter."

He stood up, immediately moving to stand by the door, his face taking on a disinterested expression as he resumed the sentry position. "Let's go for a walk. We can talk by the stream."

Her stomach churned, a mixture of morning sickness and disgust at what she would have to tell him. Knowing he'd find out eventually, she sighed deeply, resigned to speak words she didn't know she could say.

"I can't go for a walk today. I don't feel well." She looked up into his face; saw the concern that swirled within the depths of his eyes. Whisper soft, she confessed, "I think I'm pregnant." She lowered her legs over the bed and wrapped her arms tightly around her stomach. "Oh, God, I'm going to bring that bastard's child into the world."

"Or mine."

He'd spoken so quietly, she wasn't sure she'd heard him. Her blue eyes shining bright with tears, she looked up at his face, her heart breaking to see realization darkening his gaze. Just slightly, her head shook, disbelief consuming her, driving her farther into despair.

He blinked...once – twice...and his tone was curt when he finally said, "Lay down, get some sleep, and see if you feel better when you wake up. If you can, we're going out to the stream. We need to talk."

Before she could argue, he stepped into the hall and shut the door. She wasn't angry at his brevity, and she knew that his reaction would have been different if they'd not been in the house. But he was right, they did need to talk, and she hoped she'd feel up to it after she got some rest. With eyes burning, she lay back on the mattress again, curling into a fetal position, her body trembling with grief while she lost herself to sleep.

. . .

They walked quickly through the woods, her stomach having settled after she slept for a few hours. Connor was tense, each muscle of his body locked, his defensive posture apparent in his gait. He didn't move faster than she could follow and he still stopped to assist her over top roots and other obstacles that littered the path. The sky was covered in clouds again and she worried that rain could fall at any time while they made their way farther out into the woods. Small bits of light streamed in from where the leaves were less dense above their heads.

When they finally reached the stream, he led her to a large rock that sat along the edge, holding her hand until she was sitting down. "I'm fine, Connor. You don't need to start treating my like I'm fragile so early. I'll need more help when I'm so big I can't see my toes anymore" She attempted levity to try and lighten the mood that weighed down his shoulders, but he didn't crack even a slight smile in response to her words.

Intently, he stared down at her when he said, "I'm getting you out of here, Arianna. We're leaving tonight." Moving from her side, he ran his hands through his hair and began pacing back and forth along the edge of the stream.

"How will we get out? Where will we go? No. It's insane; we can't do this. We don't even know for sure that I'm pregnant..."

154

"Are you late?" He turned to her suddenly, the green of his eyes shining brilliantly in the sunlight.

"Yes," she admitted quietly.

"Then we're leaving." Stepping towards her, he grabbed her arms, pulling her closer into him, hugging her while resting his head on top of her head. Her body shook against him, sobs escaping her throat.

"We can't, Connor. It won't work. Just getting out will be dangerous, but after that, what will we do? He'll find us, and I don't even want to think about what he would do to us if we were caught." He held her tightly, and when he didn't respond she added, "It could be his child, as much as yours."

"I don't care. I'm not letting that monster anywhere near you again. I shouldn't have let it go on this long. I know the risks, but I can't sit idly and not try."

She was sick of crying, of the constant state of futility in which they lived. But she knew agreeing to leaving was risking his life. Her heart beat rapidly and her voice cracked when she said, "It's too much of a risk. I can't - I won't do it." Breathing deeply, she begged, "Connor, you need to leave. You can get out of here and he won't look for you, he has no need to keep you here, but you know if I leave, he won't rest until he's found me. He's insane, if he were to catch you, he'll kill you."

"It's a risk worth taking!"

She jumped in response to his raised voice and shame instantly appeared in his features when he looked down at her. "I'm sorry. I didn't mean to...fuck!" Letting her go, he walked away again and what was left of her already broken heart was crushed into dust as she watched him struggle with their fate.

Quietly, purposefully, she suggested, "Let's give it some time. You can figure out a way, a plan that would help us leave, possibly someone who'd be willing to help. However, leaving here tonight, with nothing but anger and rage to shelter us, that would be suicide. You have to agree with me on that, Connor. It's the only reason we've stayed as long as we have."

He stopped pacing, but didn't turn to look at her. His eyes remained locked on the water and the distant field that spread out before them. "I will find a way Arianna, I don't know how long it will take, but I will find a way."

Chapter Sixteen

Futility. Hopelessness. Impotence. Those were the only words to describe their life. After the day by the stream, Connor worked quickly in an attempt to find a way to not only escape the Estate, but to remain hidden after they'd accomplished it. However, barriers and roadblocks were all he could find. The Estate's reach was far and deep. Connor had to be careful regarding the people he approached, and even when he could find a person who would not report back to Joseph Carmichael, they refused from fear of being caught. Had it just been Connor, the chances would have been better, but as soon as it was mentioned that he intended on taking Joseph's wife with him, most people would refuse.

When Arianna's symptoms were discovered by Joseph, he'd immediately hired a midwife to assist her for the duration of the pregnancy. Connor and Arianna were never left alone, and she was specifically restricted from leaving the mansion. Security in the right wing was heightened and Joseph's appearances became more frequent. The only blessing that could be gained from the discovery that she was pregnant was that Joseph's abuse stopped and Arianna was not subjected to the degradation to which she'd become accustomed.

As Arianna grew larger, and when the baby inside her moved, her love for that child grew with her expanding waistline, and she couldn't care which man had sired the child. She spent more time in the music room, playing to the developing child in her womb, wondering if she'd be given a son or daughter. Over the months of her pregnancy, she'd written a song for the child. She'd intended for the song to be happy, to express the love she had for the person she'd someday meet, but the melody had come out sad and hauntingly beautiful instead. Secretly, she'd given the music to Connor after it had been completed and he took it, had it transcribed and penned under a fake name, returning it to her as a present for the child that was to come.

"Push!"

Her legs spread wide, Arianna's teeth clenched to the point of fracturing while the midwife sat positioned to assist with the birth. She'd been in labor for seven hours, had writhed atop the blankets of her bed, while Joseph paced at the foot. His presence sickened her, and although the midwife had told him it would be hours until the child was born, he'd refused to leave. Playing the role of the concerned husband, he made Arianna's stomach turn. Every touch, each caress, every offer of assistance or comfort caused her to flinch away from the monster she knew was hidden beneath the caring façade.

Bringing her knees up, bearing herself to the midwife, she pushed down with her body, forcing the child out into the cold air of the room. Pain unlike anything she'd known, tore through her center, made her feel like she was being ripped in two as the child progressed downwards.

When the midwife announced that the child's head could be seen, Joseph stopped pacing and leaned against the opposite wall to watch as the baby emerged. Grey eyes alight with anticipation, he smiled when the baby's head was exposed, and his eyes beamed when it was finally discovered that the child was a boy.

Falling back into the sweat soaked pillow, tears ran from Arianna's eyes at the announcement. She was thankful she could hide the true reason for her tears beneath the guise of pain. When the baby wailed, a small cry that spoke of life and health, Arianna silently apologized to the child, and prayed for the future of a soul born into damnation.

After the boy had been cleaned, the midwife handed him to Joseph swaddled in a small blue blanket. The sight was unnerving; Joseph lovingly caressed the child's head with hands that had been used for torture and abuse. The midwife stayed long enough to deliver the final remnants of the pregnancy and to clean Arianna enough so that she could comfortably lie back on the bed. When they were finally left alone, Joseph approached her holding the small child in his arms.

"He's beautiful, Arianna, just as I always knew he would be." Awestruck and proud, Joseph's tone of voice reminded her of who he'd been years before, the quality grating against her nerves. When he approached, she peeked out from under her lashes to see a shock of black hair on the child's head. Reaching down, he placed the child in her arms, small sounds escaping from out of the blanket he was wrapped within. Tears streaming down her cheeks, she reached over to carefully pull the blanket from the child's face, love becoming an inferno in her heart to look on the small features that faced her. She smiled sadly. The baby's eyes were clenched tight against the light in the room, but when they opened, Arianna's heart sank. Staring back at her, unfocused and newly born, were eyes the color of steel, shimmering silver that confirmed without a doubt who had been his father.

"He has my eyes." Standing beside her, Joseph wrung one hand over the other as he stared down at his son. "What will we name him?"

Surprised that he'd asked, Arianna looked up at the proud father before returning her eyes to the child in her arms. "I thought of some names during the pregnancy. I was thinking, if it was a boy, we'd name him Aaron."

"So similar to your name," Joseph instantly noted.

"Yes." Her heart shattered when she was sure Joseph would refuse the name.

"Aaron Joseph Carmichael," he mused. "It's a strong name, proud, like his father. I'll announce his birth this afternoon."

She looked up at him, partly relieved that he'd allow the name she'd chosen, but mostly sickened by his presence in her room. Looking over his once handsome face, she noticed how he'd lost weight, how his skin had grown pallor from whatever it was he did while in the west wing. While she stared at Joseph, the child stirred, turning its head towards her breast in search of milk. Immediately, she opened her robe and offered her breast to the child, wincing when he latched on, but delighting in the small suckling sounds he made while he ate.

"I must leave now, Arianna. Business never stops, even when a child is born." Joseph's heavy footsteps sounded as he made his way to the bedroom door. Stopping when he reached the door, he refused to look in her direction when he said, "You've proven yourself useful for once. Perhaps this can be a new beginning, now that you've learned to behave and to give me what I want."

She didn't respond, didn't release the anger she felt at the words he'd spoken. Silence permeated the air when he finally opened the door and disappeared into the hallway.

. . .

"Tonight."

One word, spoken softly so that only she could hear it. Sitting at her piano, her eyes looked across the room at the bassinet that cradled Aaron. Almost every day she brought the child into the music room, serenading him with the music she'd written for him. She marveled at how he calmed immediately to hear it. Even on days where he cried for no reason, desperately seeking sleep or comfort, but not finding it, the music would always grant him peace. She wondered if it had been due to her playing when she'd been pregnant with him. Regardless of the reason, Aaron loved to hear her play, would settle immediately when the hammer of the piano fell upon its string and the first, solitary note sounded.

Connor stood sentry behind her. His back to the door, his hands folded behind his back. Due to the increased activity in the right wing, he'd been excused from guarding her often and he'd had more time to leave the property, to seek out help from those who'd be willing to hide them from the ever-watchful eyes of Joseph.

She didn't need to ask what he meant, although she'd hoped that when he discovered to whom the child belonged, he would give up the fantastical idea of ever escaping their hellish prison. The stakes were higher now that Aaron had been born. If Connor's abduction of Joseph's wife had been unimaginable, his ability to steal Joseph's son was unthinkable and impossible - the minute chance that Joseph would have given

162

up in his search for them was completely destroyed now that his son was added to the equation.

"You're insane, Connor. There is no way. I've begged you before, and I continue to beg: Please, if you love me, please leave. Give up the idea that there is any chance for us and save yourself."

Spinning on the bench so that she could face him, Arianna looked up into green eyes, resolute and determined in his belief that they had any chance of escaping together.

"You must realize that he'll never stop searching. We'd live in hiding every day of our life; in fear that someone will someday discover us and turn us in for reward or merit."

Refusing to listen to her, Connor demanded, "Pack things for Aaron and yourself. I've found people who are willing to help; another network that Joseph all but destroyed when The Estate was built. They're small, but they won't turn us in to him. Their hatred runs as deep as ours."

"So, we'll be leaving one hell only to bury ourselves within another. What's to keep them from subjecting us to the same nightmare?" Her blue eyes glistened in the low light of the room while she attempted to introduce logic into the true helplessness of their situation. "At least here, Aaron will not be harmed. Joseph cares too much for an heir to allow anything to happen to him..."

"And what about you?"

His interruption annoyed her, knowing that his sudden response indicated her words had failed to alter what he'd planned.

"That remains to be seen. He's found me useful as a mother to his son, in the chain he's attached to me now that we share a child. He hasn't started the abuse again in the three months since Aaron's been born. Maybe..."

"That's because he carries out his sick fantasies on the women who service the west wing. I've heard the men talking. He's killed, Arianna, he's taken his tastes too far. His constant drug use is pushing him to do things no man would normally do. There's nothing keeping him from carrying out the same acts on you." Twisting from disgust, Connor's expression darkened when he thought about the activities of the west wing. "His men encourage him, act with him, and the bodies of the whores are tossed aside, burned; nothing more than garbage."

Arianna wasn't sure what bothered her more: the fact that her husband had fallen so far, or the fact that she wasn't surprised to hear it. Her eyes fell to the floor. "It'll never work, Connor. We won't succeed. Attempting it will be your death."

"You have to let me try."

Bringing her eyes back to his, she smiled sweetly at him, distraught over how unfair her life had turned out to be. "Is there really a chance? Not fantasy, not something that might occur, but something that is almost certain?"

He nodded, anticipation gracing his features that he'd convinced her to leave.

She knew she wouldn't be able to stop him and it broke her heart to think of what would occur if he failed. "Fine. I'll pack a few things tonight. If he doesn't show up, we can try."

Chapter Seventeen

Arianna stood in her bedroom, her eyes looking out the window that was opaque from the black of night. Her heart raced in her chest as sweat broke out on her skin. Aaron lay sleeping in his crib, thankfully peaceful on a night where his silence was a necessity. After agreeing to Connor's plan, she'd not asked for details on how he intended to carry it out. Instead, she played for her son until it was time to return to her suite to wait and see if Joseph would appear.

She'd secretly hoped Joseph would appear, thought that maybe his presence would buy her more time to convince Connor to give up his plan, to leave her and Aaron to whatever fate they had in the mansion.

However, midnight had come and gone and she knew Joseph had chosen to remain in the west wing. On the nights he did appear, he always did so early in the evening, acting the loving father he wanted people to believe that he was. He'd spread word of Aaron's arrival all over the network, had held a party in celebration without forcing Arianna to attend. That night, she could hear music wafting down the corridors between her suite and the ballroom and she cried to know that it was criminals who celebrated the birth of her son.

The silence of her bedroom disturbed her. Her footsteps against the stone tile sounded like a clock counting down the hour until she'd know if they would be able to escape. Connor had seemed so sure, so determined that she couldn't help the small bit of hope that had blossomed in her chest. She didn't want that hope, didn't welcome the bit of light that would cause more pain if it were extinguished.

When she heard the familiar sound of metal against metal, she turned to the door, her heart plunging into her stomach when Connor peeked around the door and entered the room. Closing it behind him, he stood silently, both looking at each other as if their last moments on Earth dangled before them.

Connor was dressed in all black as usual, the material of his t-shirt pulled tightly across his shoulders, folding the material at the ends where it stretched. His physique unhidden by his clothes, she allowed her eyes to travel over him, the memory of their one encounter in the cave replaying itself in her head.

"It's time."

Her eyes closed at his words and her heart felt like it would beat through her skin. She felt dizzy from her fear, adrenaline rushing through her veins like a turbulent flood. She moved to the closet to grab her bags, but Connor took them from her hands before she could even step back into the room. Hidden within the shadow of the closet, he peered down at her. In their continued silence she could see the same emotions brushing over her features that she had battering the walls of her body. His hand came up to her chin, one finger placed beneath it when he lifted her face to his. Whispering so that only she could hear, he said, "I know you're scared. I know you think what we are about to do is impossible, but I promise you Arianna, that it can be done. As soon as we are beyond the walls of The Estate we will be escorted away, hidden in a place where Joseph will never think to look."

He lowered his head and took her mouth softly with his. But, when he went to pull away, she reached up and tangled her fingers in his hair, pulling him into a deeper kiss filled with pain, desperation, longing and fear. Only when she'd run out of air and had to breath, did she let him go. A single tear escaped her eye and he reached up to wipe it away.

"This isn't goodbye, beautiful. It's the beginning, not the end."

Forcing herself to smile, she nodded her agreement, even though her mind wouldn't let her believe they would succeed.

Taking her hand, Connor pulled her out into the bedroom and grabbed a heavy blanket off the bed. He lifted Aaron out of the crib, careful not to jostle the sleeping child, and wrapped the blanket around him. After handing Aaron to Arianna, he opened the window and tossed her bags out into the dead of night.

Before crawling out he turned back to her and instructed, "Stay with me at all times. We'll keep to the shadows of the mansion until we can move out into the tree line. Stay as low to the ground as you can. Once we are hidden by the trees, we'll need to move quickly toward the front walls." He paused, not wanting to admit what his plan entailed. Remorsefully, he added, "I'll have to kill whatever men we come across. If you see me pull my knife, look away."

Her stomach turned at the thought of the certain violence to come. She loathed that Connor would have to commit it, but knew that it could not be avoided. When she looked to him without response he nodded his head and crawled out the large window. Reaching back in he took Aaron from her arms, assisted her through the window and handed him back to her once she was on the other side. Quickly grabbing her bags, he guided her through the shadows of the house, before reaching a point where he indicated for her to bend down and run across the grass lawn that led out into the woods.

. . .

Joseph's eyelids hung heavily over his steel grey gaze. In and out of focus, the haze of the drug he injected only minutes before slithered through his veins, bringing blessed numbness to his body and mind. It wasn't enough to disable him; he preferred smaller doses that would calm the chaos of his thoughts while still allowing him the ability to control his surroundings.

Sitting on a couch in the living room of the suite that, through the years, served as his quarters, he watched the brunette woman before him, her naked body dancing seductively to the music being pumped through the room. He imagined the things he would do that body, his eyes looking over the healthy weight to her breasts, and the muscular curve to her abdomen. When she rotated around, his eyes found her ass – round, yet firm. She was young; most likely barely twenty, but age had never been a factor to him, he'd found that women were all the same, a body to use for his pleasure and nothing more. He never found satisfaction with the women he fucked, his release a bleak drizzle compared to what it had been when he'd been with his wife. But, he couldn't touch her, not while his son was young and still depended on her for food and comfort. He feared he'd lose control with her like he had countless women; destroying her in his quest to find his release, to feed the violence that saturated every cell of his body. Rage had found him throughout the years and he'd surrendered to it without knowledge or thought, without so much as a struggle against the thing that was slowly destroying him.

The other men in attendance laughed and hollered, but it didn't draw Joseph's attention away from the dancing woman. He imagined her chained to his bed, her body swollen from lust and the pain he would deliver. His cock swelled at the thought of when they'd fought against him. He relished the feel of their nails sliding down his back, the way they screamed when he forced himself inside them, ripping the skin from his girth. It empowered him; his need to dominate only truly fed when they tried to refuse him. His tastes had started out with the willing, women who submitted easily without a fight, who had enjoyed being used, being objectified. But when the sadistic side to him reared its ugly head, when they'd been exposed to the level of pain Joseph preferred to impart, that's when he found the only thing that could fulfill his ever-increasing need for control.

The woman's eyes met his, a honey brown that carried no intelligence within its hue. She was obviously drugged, a state of euphoria alight on her face and when she discovered that he'd been watching her, a smile cracked the corners of her full lips, an invitation extended for him to take what he wanted. He cock twitched and he motioned for the girl to walk over to where he sat. She smiled brighter, delighted to gain his acceptance. Prowling over to him, she stopped when she stood between his parted legs. His hand reached up to her and he pulled her down to kneel in front of him. When she settled on the floor, he reached out, taking her breast in his hand before bending over to take the taut peak between his lips. His tongue flicked out to lave across the swollen bud before he took it between his teeth and bit down.

When she half cried and half moaned, his pants tightened more, and he reached down with his other hand and found the moist heat between her thighs. His fingers pushed within the soft skin, until he forced them up inside her body. Her hips undulated over his hand and her muscles gripped him hungrily. Pulling away from her, he sat back, looking to her to satisfy him before he could take her to his bed. She watched as he spread his arms across the back of the couch, his legs spread wide in invitation for her touch.

She giggled, realization dawning on her as to what he was demanding and she immediately reached out to unbuckle his belt and unzip his pants. Pulling him free of the material, her eyes widened at his size, heat and anticipation lighting her gaze when she leaned forward to take him into her mouth.

His head fell back against the leather, but he kept his eyes turned downwards so he could watch the bounce to her breasts as she moved up and down, her tongue running along his length, her lips growing even more full as she took him impossibly deep. Her actions weren't enough to get him off, the violence missing from the encounter, but it was enough to get him started, to rev up the engines to a point where he'd drag her back to his room.

When her hands found his balls and she massaged over the skin, his hips bucked. His heart sped up delivering another rush of the drug he'd earlier ingested and he didn't notice

172

when Emory marched into the room. It was only when the couch sunk beneath him from Emory's weight that he looked over to his first guard.

"We have a problem, Joseph. One that requires immediate action." Emory's tone was agitated, yet excited.

One eyebrow arched over Joseph's eye and he straightened slightly, waiting for Emory to continue.

"Connor is attempting to flee the compound."

Joseph chuckled, unsure why Emory was concerned about Connor. "He's not a prisoner, he can come and go as he pleases. Although I'm not pleased that he left Arianna and Aaron alone in the suite." Joseph's hand reached down and rested on the head of the woman between his legs. He guided her faster along his cock, needing the increasing speed and pressure to keep him from going soft."

"That's the thing, Joseph. He hasn't left them. He's attempting to take them with him. One of the men you have stationed outside her window saw them and they've been followed into the woods."

The woman screamed when Joseph's fingers tangled furiously into her hair. Ripping her off of him, he tossed her to the floor, kicking her away from his feet when he refastened his pants. She crawled away like a dog, shame turning her

173

cheeks red when the other men in the room laughed at what Joseph had done.

Joseph's fury boiled within his veins; betrayed by his guard and his wife, he saw red before his eyes, thought of nothing but death when he considered what he had to do.

Making a decision, he stood suddenly, and looked down at Emory, his voice took on a commanding tone when he ordered, "Gather every man in my personal guard, have them meet at the front gates. I want someone guarding every possible exit along the walls. Keep this quiet, Emory, I don't need the entire network knowing what my wife has done."

Emory turned to carry out Joseph's order and Joseph added, "Tell the men that follow them not to approach. Connor's nothing if not lethal, they won't stand a chance against him alone." A sick smile stretching across his face he added, "Plus, I want our reunion to be a surprise."

Chapter Eighteen

The fallen branches breaking beneath their feet were the only sound they could hear as they moved through the forest. Connor wanted to move faster, but Arianna was unable to keep up, the babe in her arms heavy after carrying it while attempting to navigate the top roots and low lying plants that blocked their path.

It was a moonless night and Arianna struggled to keep her eyes focused against the consuming darkness that surrounded them. She wasn't sure how Connor knew where to go when their sight was impeded by the thickness of night.

When the lights of the front wall came into view, Arianna's heart raced faster. She knew that they would have to approach the gates, knew that there were men who stood guard at the entrance. Connor knelt down when the lights came into view, pulling Arianna down to his side as he looked out over the lawn to the wall on the far side. Leaning over so that he could whisper in her ear, his lips tickled along the lobe when he said, "We're going to have to move quickly across the field. Once we approach the wall, there is a good three feet of shadow from the way the lights are situated on top. Stick to that area,

Arianna. Even when we reach the guards he has stationed along the walls, don't move out from the shadows. If I have to fight, stay put until I've taken him down. Do you understand?"

She nodded, fear apparent in her eyes as she looked up into his. His features softened, his face falling down so he could brush his lips softly across hers. "We'll be fine, I promise you. I love you Arianna, there's nothing I wouldn't do for you."

It was a punch to the chest, to hear those words spoken to her by the man she'd grown attached to over the time that she'd known him. Love. Such a simple word that carried more meaning that any other she knew. Her heart skipped at the thought that he'd become her guardian, her savior in a world where there'd been no hope.

"I love you too." Her voice choked on the emotion ravaging her body, the elation mixed with dread, anticipation thickened with fear.

He smiled allowing the dimples to appear on his cheeks adding the boyish look to his face that she'd enjoyed in the rare moments they'd been happy.

Gripping her around her elbow, Connor guided her from beneath the trees out to the yard that stretched out before them. Keeping low to the ground, they reached the shadowed area within seconds, catching their breath before proceeding along the perimeter of the wall.

All appeared quiet, but when they heard the slight crush of grass against feet, Arianna looked over Connor's shoulder and winced to see three men standing at attention along the wall. Arianna stopped suddenly and watched helplessly as Connor turned to her and indicated for her to be quiet before he moved to sneak up behind the men. She noticed that Aaron stirred in her arms and she softly swayed him back and forth, in an attempt to goad him back into a deep sleep.

Connor moved quickly, a shadow himself as he sped towards the men. She watched as he pulled the knife from the sheath at his back, reaching up and running it along the neck of the first man he approached. The man he'd grabbed dropped lifelessly to the ground, his head almost completely severed from his shoulders. The other two men turned instantly in Connor's direction, and were quickly silenced when he pulled a second blade, sinking one into the temple of one and into the top of the head of the other. Her eyes held wide, she continued to watch as he allowed their bodies to fall to the ground, placing his foot onto the shoulder of one in order to free his blade from the man's skull.

Dizziness from what she'd seen weakened her knees and she fell back along the stone surface of the wall, closing her eyes to the gore that littered their path. She could hear Connor moving about and when she finally felt a hand on her shoulder, she jumped, but opened her eyes to find his perfect emerald gaze staring back at her.

Whispering, he asked, "Are you okay?"

She swallowed the lump that was stuck in her throat, and nodded her head 'yes' to his inquiry. He looked her over for another second, before gripping her elbow to lead her farther along the wall.

They ran into two more teams of men, each one quickly dispatched and dragged away by Connor. When she finally spied the front of the mansion and when her eyes were met with the large iron gates, relief started tickling along her spine. A man stepped out of the shadow in the distance and Connor stopped suddenly, reaching back to push her lower to the ground as he knelt down. Their combined breathing was heavy, her heart beating so frantically she feared she would pass out from the rush of blood it induced.

The surrounding area was deathly quiet except for the hushed voices of three men that stood guard at the gate. Connor turned to Arianna, a smile peaking out from his lips. "This should be simple enough. Once we are past those gates, we'll only have to travel a little while longer before we will be picked up and transported to another home."

She smiled back, the small bit of hope she'd allowed, now blossoming in its depth.

"Stay here. Let me go deal with our friends up ahead and I'll come back to grab you when they've been removed. We're going to make it, try not to worry."

Quickly, she pushed up to kiss him once more before he disappeared into the darkness to kill the final guards that stood in their path. A few minutes passed and she grew worried. Sitting against the wall, she clutched Aaron to her chest, her mind repeating a prayer that Connor return unharmed. A hand fell on her shoulder and she jumped from surprise, but smiled again to be met with Connor's face. "It's done. We're leaving here finally."

Grabbing her by the elbow, he helped her stand with Aaron still clutched tightly to her chest. They moved silently through the shadow, her heartbeat the only thing she could hear besides the pound of Connor's boots. Reaching the large iron gate, he pushed the button to open it and turned to smile at her as the creak of the hinges announced their escape from the hell they'd been living for years.

Arianna smiled brightly, fear still alive in her heart but quickly smothered by the feeling of happiness that came with their success. She couldn't believe how easy it had been and she felt stupid for not having attempted it before now. Shaking herself of those thoughts, she bundled Aaron in one arm and reached out to take Connor's hand. He pulled her into his side, the warmth of his body chasing away the chill of the night air on hers and when the gate parted enough to let them pass, he kissed her on the forehead before saying, "It's time, beautiful."

Striding out quickly, they moved past the gates and once outside the walls, Arianna looked away from Connor's face and found the sickening smile across Emory's.

Arianna gasped and faltered in her step, moving back away from the two men when Connor jumped to attack Emory. Connor moved to stab Emory in the temple and quickly kill him as he did the others, but when Emory moved suddenly, Connor's knife caught the side of his face and dragged along the skin, opening his cheek to the point where muscle was split and bone was exposed. Her stomach twisting from the sight, she continued stepping away until she felt her back press up against a warm body and arms reaching around to grab not only her, but also Aaron.

She pulled away instantly; not knowing who had grabbed her and when she heard Joseph's wicked chuckle sound behind her, her heart fell and her knees weakened to realize escape had not been as easily gained as they'd believed.

Her eyes still locked to Connor and Emory while they fought, they widened to see additional men stepping out from the shadows beyond the wall. At least twenty men appeared and moved in to assist Emory. Connor noticed the additional men immediately, spinning quickly to fight, his blades finding their way across the throats of those who moved too close. He fought valiantly, his strength and speed obvious in the movements of his body, but with the number of men who attacked, it became bleakly apparent that he'd been outnumbered.

When the men had finally contained him and had stripped him of his weapons, they forced him to his knees facing Arianna. He looked up, one eye red and swelling from where he'd been hit, his bottom lip stained from where it had been split.

Tears falling from her face, she felt Joseph lean down and his lips brush across her ear. His breath rolled along her skin and every muscle tensed at its contact. Pain, absolute and unadulterated tore at her chest, her sobs breaking free of her body when realization of what was to come touched her thoughts.

"Do you think it's so easy to escape me? To run off like a whore into the night with a guard? I thought you were better than that, my love." The last words were laced with venom, his hatred for her apparent in the lethal edge to his voice.

She didn't dare look at him, couldn't bring herself to look away from Connor who kept his emerald gaze locked to her in sorrow and defeat. Emory stepped out from around the men, blood pouring out from his cheek where Connor had torn it open. Emory indicated for the men to lift Connor and when he was back on his feet, Emory punched him in the gut, causing Connor to bend over in pain. Bringing his fist up, Emory caught Connor in the chin and blood spewed from his mouth from the force of the hit.

Arianna cried harder. She knew they would kill him, would beat him to death before her eyes. Her body shook violently with fear and bitterness, waking Aaron from his slumber until he cried out. The small sound broke her heart even more when she feared what would happen to her child now that they'd been caught.

"Stop!" Joseph's voice boomed out into the silent night sky and Emory stepped away from Connor. His face was deformed from where Emory had broken bones and his body hung helplessly, only remaining standing because of the guards that held him.

Joseph removed one arm from Arianna and motioned one of the men over to where they stood. "Take my son. I have a lesson that needs to be taught to these traitors."

Her body tensed impossibly tighter and she attempted to fight against the man who reached for the screaming child, but her efforts were made useless when Joseph grabbed her arms and forced her to let go. Her eyes only left Connors when they moved to follow the man who held her child, not knowing if it would be the last time she ever saw her son.

With Aaron screaming in the background, Joseph pushed Arianna towards Connor, letting them stand within a few short feet of each other when he finally spoke again.

"I'm disappointed, Connor, I could have sworn you knew better than this." Joseph's hands moved up to Arianna's shirt, his fingers finding the first button of her blouse, undoing it slowly

182

while keeping his eyes trained on Connor. Anger poured into Connor's stare and Arianna attempted to pull away from her husband. Joseph grabbed her, his fingers digging so far into her skin, it caused her to cry out in pain. Losing his sense of delicacy, Joseph reached around with the other hand, ripping open her shirt, exposing her breasts to the men that stood before them. "Is this what you wanted? The flesh of another man's wife?"

Joseph's hand rubbed up her torso, eventually cupping the weight of her breast before tightly pinching the peak between his fingers. She cried out from the pain, tears breaking free of her eyes as her husband reached down again to remove her pants. His eyes still locked to Connor, Joseph continued ripping her clothes away until she stood naked and exposed to the group of men who held her guard.

Connor struggled against the men who held him, but was met with the fist of another who stood nearby. More blood burst from his mouth, before that same man grabbed his hair and forced his eyes up to watch Joseph and Arianna.

Quiet laughter sounded behind her, and Joseph released her breast to run his hand down along her stomach eventually settling his touch between her legs, rubbing his finger along the sensitive bundle of nerves. One finger pushing down through the flesh, he tsked. "She's become wet for my touch but, I'll allow you to watch this time, to see what you could have had if you'd been a better man."

Forcing Arianna to her knees, Joseph pushed her head forward against the ground. She could hear Connor struggle again, only to be met with the sickening crunch of another fist against his body. When Joseph had removed his pants, he rubbed the hard length of his cock along the folds of her skin, forcing himself painfully inside her. She screamed, the flesh ripping from the intrusion, burning as he held her hips still with one hand and her face to the ground with the other. The white noise of rushing blood pulsed through her head, her eyes locked to Connor's as Joseph pumped himself in and out forcefully. The men quieted and Arianna shrank at the sounds of Joseph pleasuring himself with her body, embarrassing her while grunting above her. She could see the seething anger in Connor's gaze; only one eye left open, and the other swollen painfully shut.

Joseph roared out his release, his fingers digging into the flesh of her hips and tearing hair away from her scalp. Her mouth opened on a silent scream, bits of dirt and grass caught on her lips from where her face had been shoved to the ground. When he finished, Joseph kicked out with his foot, the sole making contact with her ass as she was shoved to the ground once more. She lay still, not wanting to move; too afraid to do anything that could cause Joseph to lose control.

When the night had grown quiet except for Aaron's wail, Joseph moved in front of Connor. One face to another, Joseph spit at Connor before bringing his fist to Connor's gut and his knee to

Connor's face. The crack of bone echoed out across the walls of the compound accompanied by the sickening chuckle of the men in response.

"Take him back to the mansion. I'll deal with my wife."

The men moved to comply with Joseph's instruction and Joseph turned to kneel down where Arianna still lay on the ground.

"And you..." He shook his head, tsking again in mockery of her shame and pain. "Apparently you still haven't learned what happens when you betray me." His hand reached down, his fingers tangling painfully into her hair and her body moved across the ground, dragged by a hand that threatened to tear the skin from her skull as he pulled her along the grass behind him.

Chapter Nineteen

Arianna rested on the large king sized bed in her room. Her body hurt from the bruises and cuts along her arms, torso and legs. Three days had passed since she'd been caught at the gates with Connor, three days where Joseph had attacked her every day and every night, leaving her broken and spent, but not so crushed that she couldn't tend to Aaron.

Joseph was not a stupid man. He understood the need of an infant to have a mother close by, and Joseph did not trust Aaron in anyone's hands besides Arianna. He knew that she'd care for the child, that she loved him and would protect him even if her heart was filled with hate for his father.

Chained to her bed, Arianna was only released on the occasion where she needed to go to the bathroom or shower. She was given enough length to easily reach her son and food and water were brought to her three times daily. What little freedom she had before her attempted escape had been stripped from her, replaced with the reality that she served one purpose alone – to care for the son of a monster. Having lost Connor as a guard, Joseph quickly replaced him with four other men, strict orders given to each that they were not to approach or speak to Arianna unless another man was present.

Even though she fought to keep her mind from thoughts of Connor's fate, she couldn't help but wonder what they'd done to him. She knew Joseph was cruel, that he'd probably ordered the death of the man she loved and she feared that the method of death had been unforgiving and brutal. Tears fell from her swollen eyes for the loss of the only man who'd helped her in the nightmare in which she lived.

Having fallen asleep, she was awoken by the click of her door as it opened, the scream of the hinges against the stillness of her room. Her eyes peeked open, and she watched Joseph step inside. He crossed the room to look in on Aaron, a smile touching the sides of his lips to see his child sleeping peacefully within the crib. That smile faded, however, when he turned and allowed his eyes to travel along the length of Arianna's body. She flinched when he approached and she tried to scoot away from him on the mattress when he sat down.

"I have an event you must attend tonight. I don't like leaving Aaron in another person's care, but it can't be avoided given the circumstances. It should only take an hour or so, and there's no need for you to dress appropriately for what's to come."

Her heart pounded into her throat, her stomach threatening to relieve itself of the dinner she'd eaten a few hours before. Not moving an inch, she opened her mouth, attempting to speak clearly between lips that were busted and raw from where Joseph had struck her across the face. Her throat burned and her tongue felt swollen when she asked, "Where are you taking me?"

She wasn't sure she wanted an answer to her question, couldn't fathom what Joseph had staged for her to see.

Joseph smiled sweetly, bits of the man he'd been years ago peeking out from behind the cold, dead stare of his eyes. His hand reached out to brush her hair from her face and she instinctively recoiled from his touch.

"Now, Arianna, there's no need to fear me. I've done nothing wrong. You've asked for everything that's happened to you. I've been nothing but a good husband; keeping a roof over your head, food in your stomach and clothes on your back. I even gave you a guard to protect you, and what do you do? Try and sneak off with him – to take my son from me?" His words were dreadfully calm, almost happy and satisfied in their tone. "But after tonight, I won't have to worry about that anymore. You'll love me again, without the confusion of another man's interest."

Her heart felt like it would explode, and she became sick when realization dawned as to what he was telling her. Finding the strength to speak again, she pushed herself up from the bed, crawling closer to her husband, begging, "Please,

Joseph, whatever you have planned, I don't want to be a part of it. Please. I'll do anything, just don't…"

He shushed her, the comforting sound perverted by the ill intent of the man who made it. "Anything?" He brought his finger to his lip, tapping it while pretending to be deep in thought. Standing up, he reached down with his hand, "Come with me, I have an idea."

There was no trust in her for the man that stood before her, but without a choice, she stood as instructed, taking his hand when he attempted to assist her. Letting her go only briefly, he bent over to remove the shackle from her ankle, a hiss escaping her lips when the cool air met with the skin that had been opened by the rough circle of metal.

Taking her hand again, he led her into the bathroom, closing the door behind them with a soft click as she entered the low lighting of the room. She turned to him, not sure what he would ask of her, and praying if she pleased him, he wouldn't force her to participate in whatever it was he'd earlier planned.

"Tell me you love me, Arianna. Tell me how you belong to me alone, how even if you'd escaped, you would never let another man's hands touch you."

She said what he wanted to her say, fell to her knees begging forgiveness in utter desperation to avoid whatever event he'd wanted her to attend.

Pulling a chair from near the wall, he sat it down in front of the vanity, so that the back of his head was clearly visible in front of the mirror. Taking a seat, he looked over at her. She crawled to him, ready to do whatever vile thing was necessary to change his mind. Placing one finger beneath her chin, he lifted her tear-streaked face so she looked directly into his eyes. "Dance for me, beautiful, show me the way your body moves just because you're near me." He released her and sat back awaiting his show.

Her body and heart grew numb, but she pushed herself up on her feet, slowly removing her clothes before swaying her hips to music unheard. Her eyes couldn't help but look upon her image in the mirror and she winced to see the marks along her skin, the scars from years of beatings, her ribs that were exposed from lack of nutrition over the past couple of days.

The image sickened her, but she steeled her spine and danced for Joseph, attempting to goad him into satisfaction. He watched her from beneath the heavy lids of his eyes, his tongue flicking out to rub along his bottom lip. "That's right baby, remind me why I fell in love with you in the first place."

She kept dancing, fighting back tears of shame and regret while moving in front of him. When he stood suddenly, she couldn't help but flinch, fear racing along her spine at what he would do to her next. Casually he pushed the chair aside and crooked his finger for her to approach him.

When she was near enough for him to grab her, he pulled her against his chest. The smell of his cologne mixed with the ever-present smell of alcohol burned at her nostrils. His mouth to her ear, he asked, "Do you love me?"

"Yes, Joseph, more than anything," she lied.

His chest vibrated with a deep chuckle. "And do you want to do anything to please me?"

"Yes."

He leaned down, his mouth finding hers as his tongue slid along her lips seeking entrance. She wanted to vomit, wanted to fight against the intimacy of his kiss, but instead opened her mouth, allowing him inside, acting as if she couldn't get enough of him.

Breaking apart from her he moved quickly away and instructed, "Move to the vanity. Place your hands on the counter, your ass held high for me."

She watched him in the mirror as she approached the counter. Placing her hands down she assumed the position he'd requested, her arms locked tight against whatever pain he could inflict against her. She continued watching as he approached and unbuckled his pants, letting them fall to his ankles while positioning himself behind her. One hand reached up to grab her hair, to hold her in place with her eyes locked to the mirror. He smiled again. "Don't close your eyes, beautiful, I want you to watch while I take you."

With one powerful thrust he forced himself inside her before he let go of her hair to wrap his fingers painfully around her hips. In a slow rhythm, he pounded within her, his head falling back as he groaned out his pleasure. After a few minutes, he pulled out. Locking his eyes with hers in the mirror, a grimace darkened his expression before he pushed into the tight opening of her ass. She cried out in pain, but did not remove her eyes from the image portrayed in the mirror.

"Tell me how much you like it. Tell me you want it harder."

Tears finally escaping her eyes, she said, "I love it, Joseph, I want it harder." Her voice cracked on those words but they seemed to satisfy him while he finished within her, finding his release while she watched. He pulled out, slapping her against the skin of her ass hard enough that it caused her entire body to shake from its force.

Another smile fell over his face as he moved to the shower to clean himself. When he'd finished and returned to stand behind her, he reached around and removed her hands from the counter. Bringing one hand up to his lips, he held her back against his chest and his other hand found her breast. Placing one soft kiss on her palm, he said, "Be ready in twenty minutes."

Her knees buckled and he laughed when he dropped her to the floor. Exiting the room, he turned back to her, a blank expression on his face when he said, "Emory will be here to retrieve you shortly. I'd get dressed if you want to save what little dignity you have left."

Chapter Twenty

Her feet hit painfully against the stone tile of the hallway as Emory led her through the corridor leading to the ballroom. When they approached the large double doors, Arianna expected the guards to open them for her to enter, but instead, they stood still, barely looking at her as she approached. She stopped in front of the doors, only looking back at Emory when his hand grabbed her neck to turn her towards the mansion's foyer. Confusion filled her mind, but she dutifully stepped forward, not daring to upset the man behind her.

"We won't be meeting in the ballroom tonight, sweetheart. Your husband has gone out of his way to plan an event that will be more special than any that you have attended before." He laughed while walking her towards the large front doors, brushing against her when he reached around to pull the metal handle and lead them outside.

When he'd arrived to her room, it was the first time she'd seen him since that night at the gate. Her eyes immediately sought out the cut across his cheek, a sick satisfaction that it appeared several hundred stitches were needed to close up the gaping wound Connor had left on his face.

Underneath the new moon that hung sorrowfully in the sky, she walked ahead of Emory, in route towards a field that she knew existed on the opposite side of the building. As they approached the area, her eyes found a circle of torches, fire rushing angrily towards the sky where they'd been placed. Light and shadow danced along the bodies of the few men who stood on the outside of a circle set in the middle. Her brow furrowed when she saw four cars, positioned so that their rear ends were tucked within the circle.

Heads turned in her direction as she approached, and when the small group of men parted, Joseph stepped out from the center, walking towards her as she neared.

Taking her hand, he smiled at her, his eyes quickly flicking to Emory before falling back to her face. "Now that we have our honored guest in attendance, we can begin."

Her eyes shot up to his before moving to peer over his shoulder. She couldn't understand what was going on, why Joseph had staged the event outside, instead of in the ballroom. She suspected it had to do with the cars, but she couldn't imagine why they were needed or what he planned to do with them.

Joseph led her to the fire-ensconced circle, covering her eyes with his hand and laughing when she flinched at the contact. Walking her to a position where he was satisfied, he removed his hand, slowly revealing the scene that was laid out before her.

She fell back instantly, her head shaking in denial of what she saw. Her husband was insane, she knew that, but she'd never dreamed how evil he'd become. Her heart pounded so violently, she feared it would break through her sternum, her chest heaving with erratic breath, fast and shallow, in no way delivering the amount of oxygen she needed to adequately process what was going on. Her eyes immediately moved to Joseph, terror wracking her nerves until every muscle quivered under its hold.

"You c...can't do this, Joseph. P...please – please just let him go."

Joseph stood perfectly still. With his hands folded behind his back, he looked at her through wide eyes, delight dancing across the molten grey at the *event* he'd planned for her. "Oh, sweet, Arianna. You see, my darling, I can't let him go. He intended to take two things from me, both of which I held dearly to my heart." Pulling his hands out from behind his back, he lifted them as if in surrender, and shrugged his shoulders when he said, "I'm sorry, beautiful, but he's been sentenced to death."

He stalked towards her, every muscle in his body visible under the material of his crisp white shirt. Shadows and light from the fire danced across his face, casting a menacing light to an expression that already spoke of intense hatred and maniacal thoughts. When he was so close, she could smell the sweetness of the alcohol on his breath and could feel the heat that rolled off his large body, he asked, "Are you ready to find out why you're here?"

Her entire body shook, fear producing sweat that rolled off her skin, her stomach twisted into a knot at how much worse the situation would become.

Joseph reached up and snapped his fingers, and out of her periphery vision she could see Emory moving towards them, his large body somehow slithered in the manner in which he moved. When he was almost to them, Joseph grabbed Arianna's chin, lifting her face to him when his mouth covered hers, his tongue sliding across her teeth, her tongue, invading her to the point where she could barely breath.

He pulled back, his hand moving to wipe the moisture from around his lips. "My beautiful girl, you're here because you get to choose how he dies."

When Joseph backed away, Connor once again came into view. He sat on his knees in the middle of the cars, his broad chest was bare, only a pair of stained and torn sweatpants on his body to cover him. His head was bent forward, the pure black of his hair shining brightly underneath the light of the flames. Her eyes traveled over his skin, her body wracking with sobs to see the wide gashes where he'd been cut, or the bruises and deformed bones that protruded from beneath. His once-beautiful body was disfigured from the days of abuse he'd obviously endured.

"Connor, why don't you look up so you can see Arianna for the last time. She's looking absolutely lovely tonight."

Arianna's breath caught in her chest when Connor's arms shook against the chains shackled to his wrists. The muscles flexed, their lines defined by the shadows of the flames. Sweat soaked his skin and caused him to glow under the light. Slowly, he lifted his head, his swollen lids fluttering open, his emerald eyes finally peeking out at her from beneath the fan of black lashes that lined them.

Sobs broke free, her body violently shaking from their force. She wanted to drop to her knees, wanted to crawl to the man that she loved and break him free of the chains that bound him where he knelt.

Joseph moved to her side, put his arm around her waist as if he wished to steady her and prevent her from falling to the ground. "As I'm sure you figured out Arianna, Connor is about to die a somewhat quick, but very painful death."

Her eyes left Connor to travel the length of the chains that were attached to his arms and attached to the rear bumpers of the cars. She noticed two other chains that she knew had to be attached to Connor's ankles, the opposite ends also attached to the cars. "Joseph, no. This is too far, this…it'll tear him apart."

"Precisely, my beautiful wife. And I imagine a death such as that must sting a little." He mocked her with his words, acted nonchalant, as if they were talking about nothing more than the weather. "There is a way you can help him, however."

Joseph put his hand to his side, palm up so that his fingers could wrap around the handle of the blade that Emory gave him. Arianna looked down at the knife, the blade polished to a point where it flickered from the firelight above.

When her eyes finally rose up to look at Joseph, he grinned. "You can make this easy for him. All you have to do is cut his throat, or stab him in the heart. End his life for him quickly, or subject him to being ripped into four pieces.

"No, Joseph – no I can't do this." Her knees threatened to give out again, and her head hurt from the pressure of the blood rushing through her veins. She felt like her heart would stop, that she'd drop to the ground unable to move or scream, if she couldn't wake up from an event that was so horrible it couldn't be real.

"No? That's fine. We'll do it my way, then." Lifting his hand again, he snapped his fingers and the engines to the cars started in unison. She couldn't move, her jaw hanging uselessly as she stood in shock.

The cars seemed to jump when they moved forward. Slowly the slack in the chains decreased while Connor fought to keep his head up so that he could look at Arianna. Her hand went to her mouth, covering an expression of absolute horror. When the chains lifted, Connor's legs were forced out from beneath him, his body elevated off the ground from the movement of the cars. His face twisted, his jaw locked with clenched teeth, and a scream tore from his throat when his appendages were stretched taut and pulled out painfully from his body.

"STOP!!" Her throat was raw when she screamed, her eyes unable to focus from the burning pain of her tears. "Stop! Joseph, you have to stop!"

Joseph snapped again and Emory yelled out a command in response. The cars stopped, the white of their rear lights shining as they backed up and lowered Connor's body to the ground. When he was down, he writhed over the grass, extreme pain apparent by the way his muscles twitched over his bones.

Finally, not having the strength to hold herself up any longer, Arianna fell to the ground, her body folding over itself as she fell. Joseph knelt down beside her, offering the knife to her, a man in supplication. She eyed the knife warily, her eyes sliding across the sharpened blade, her hands digging into the earth beneath her.

"This is your choice, Arianna, but I'll only allow you to make it once. I've stopped the cars, I've done what you asked, but you must follow through with your part of the bargain. If you can't do it this time, I won't stop the cars again."

She reached out to take the knife from his hand. She imagined slicing it across his throat, or turning so quickly that the blade sank deeply into his heart, slicing open the cold and bitter thing that beat in his chest. But she couldn't. If she attacked him, he'd kill her and her son would be left alone, raised by monsters, made into a monster himself.

As soon as her fingers had wrapped tightly around the handle, Joseph grabbed her by her hair, forcing her ear to his mouth. "Kill him for me, my love. Prove to me that you prefer me to that man. I want to believe you didn't want to leave with him, I want to believe he'd forced you to leave."

His insanity was proven beyond doubt. Arianna knew from his words that he'd come up with excuses, lies to protect his precious ego from her betrayal. She'd known all along, but she didn't realize, could never have imagined, how depraved he'd become.

Pushing herself up from the ground, she walked slowly towards Connor. Her legs felt heavy when she walked, her torso wanting to give out, allowing her to fold back over to the ground, to ball up in protection from a waking nightmare. When she approached Connor, his eyes were clenched in pain, his face a stark white skin stretched taut over the disfigured features of his face. Dropping to her knees beside him, she fought against reaching out to touch him, to provide him even a small amount of comfort in what she was about to do.

Speaking low so that only he could hear her, she said, "I love you, Connor. I don't want to do this, but I can't let you die the other way." Her throat could barely move and her words were broken by the quake of her body.

His eyes opened and his head turned so that he could look at her. Even though his jaw looked like it was broken, he opened his mouth to talk, a single tear escaping his eyes as he looked her over once more. "You don't have to do this." His words were spoken so quietly, so slowly, that she could barely hear him. "Lo...love you. Don't let him..." The blood coughed from his lungs caused him to pause before he finished, "Don't let him do this to you. I'm...I'm sorry...for failing."

Her chest felt like it ripped open from pain. She could have plunged the knife in her own body and would have hurt less than the emotions his words made her feel. Speaking through her tears, she said, "You didn't fail. I know you did everything you could. I'm not letting him do anything, Connor, I'm doing this because I love you and because I can't let him torture you any more."

"Get on with it, Arianna! We don't have all night!" A deep baritone, the accent of a rich and powerful man, Joseph's voice echoed across the field, louder than the engines of the cars, or the murmured noises made by the other men.

Her body shook, her eyes never leaving Connor's when she leaned over his body and placed the blade to his neck. The skin of his throat moved over the steel of the blade when he instructed, "Push deep and pull hard. There are only two veins you need to cut." He paused to catch his breath before adding, "I know you love me, I know we could have been good together. We were. I'm sorry to leave you behind, Arianna." He closed his eyes and his head leaned back against the grass, awaiting his fate.

She allowed her anger towards Joseph to drive her, to provide strength to the muscle in her arm. Squeezing her eyes shut against the terror she felt, she opened them again and gritted her teeth when she dragged the blade across his neck, hard and deep just like he'd instructed. Blood shot out from the wound, streaming in pulses from his body, the beat of his heart driving the spray.

Falling back, Arianna screamed. The knife fell from her hand and she reached up, pulling at her hair in absolute misery at what Joseph had forced her to do. She watched the color drain from Connor's face, his eyes rolling beneath his eyelids while he struggled to breath. She placed her hand on his chest, felt the strength of his heart dissipate and fade, until, finally, it no longer beat beneath her hand. She didn't care if Joseph saw her touch him, she wanted to let him know she was there until the last minute, until the last bit of life was drained from his body.

Strong hands gripped around her biceps. She was lifted from the ground and held in a standing position over Connor. Warm breath trailed down her skin when Joseph leaned over to whisper in her ear. "I'm impressed, beautiful. To be honest, I never thought you'd actually do it."

She didn't respond, couldn't force her lips to move so she could tell him just how much she despised him. Every part of her body had gone numb, her mind reeling from having been forced to extinguish the flame of her lover's life.

Joseph pulled her back away from the body, but held her still when they'd retaken their previous position within the circle. Leaning down to her again, he laughed before saying, "You didn't think I'd let my men miss out on the show, did you?"

His hand raised in the air. His fingers snapped.

Her jaw dropped open when she saw the cars lurch forward and Connor's body was torn apart in midair.

Chapter Twenty-One

Three years. Three years that she'd been alone, trapped in a prison where she was beaten nightly; raped and molested when the beast that was her husband fancied her touch. She was allowed to remain in her suite in the right wing. Security was heightened; she was monitored by both cameras and the living eyes of Joseph's men. There was nowhere she could go where she wasn't watched, there was no escape from the life Joseph had built for her.

But there was a small light, a single flame that not even Joseph would extinguish, and that little boy was everything to her. Aaron grew fast, his small body becoming strong when he learned to crawl, to walk...to run. His hair remained the color of pitch black night and his skin was a natural golden tan. He had a laugh that could light up any room, and he was fearless when it came to trying new things. But his eyes; over time they'd started to change, becoming a brilliant sapphire blue by the time he was two. Joseph had noticed, but had quickly brushed it off that the child had inherited Arianna's eyes. However, when veins of green started to show from beneath the azure surface, Arianna quickly questioned everything she thought she knew.

It was a gradual change; one she hoped would stop. In her heart she was desperate to learn that they'd been wrong, that Aaron had been Connor's child and not Joseph's, but she feared what Joseph would do to Aaron if he found out. She lived in fear, each day waking to a child, looking deep in his eyes, scared senseless that she'd wake to the emerald green of Connor's eyes.

The midwife had told her that his eyes could change. She'd said it was common for children to be born with grey or blue eyes, and for those eyes to eventually turn to a lighter or darker shade as they grew older.

Sitting in her bedroom, she stared out at the red walls, not wanting to move, much less walk into a living room she knew was occupied by several of Joseph's guards. He no longer kept her chained; and he had no reason to continue locking her up. She had no spirit left in her. He'd broken her that night on the field. He'd taken something of beauty, of redemption and light and he'd made her destroy it, made her commit an act so vile, she could never forgive herself for having done it. Never again would she attempt to leave, and for the sake of Aaron, never again would she fight against the will of her husband.

She felt empty – completely lost to the insanity that permeated the walls of the house, only able to keep herself sane by caring for her son.

Joseph's depravities had worsened and death was a common occurrence each time he held a meeting within the network. He ruled his organization with an iron fist, never allowing one man to go without punishment for the smallest infraction. He enjoyed delivering his sentences, each time surprising his audience with just how sick and twisted he could become. She loathed him, loathed the network of men that worked for him, but she stood dutifully when she was called to attend the meetings, sat beside him imitating the committed wife. It kept Aaron alive. That was her only concern.

Sitting on the side of her bed, she pulled black stockings over her legs before standing up to slip a one sleeved black dress over her body. He wanted her to dress up, to have a picture made with him before he started the night's meeting. His network, his *family*, his money – those were the accomplishments he flaunted to his men, to anyone and everyone who met him. If you didn't know him, you'd think he was perfect. It was frightening how charismatic he could be when there was nothing beneath his skin but a dead heart and the soul of a demon.

She sat at her vanity, brushing her long, blonde hair, waiting for him to arrive. When she heard the click of the door handle, she turned, pushing up on to her feet so that she didn't keep him waiting. She'd learned not to anger him, to submit to every dark desire he had in order to avoid his violence, if only for a night or two. Even though he slept with her often and never used protection, she didn't become pregnant again. She was thankful for that fact, but it made her wonder even more about who had fathered her son.

"Arianna. You look beautiful. Once again, the men will envy the beauty of the woman at my side." His voice purred, anticipation heightening his spirits for the meeting that was to come.

She smiled in response, always playing the perfect wife. "Thank you, Joseph. You look handsome as usual." Her eyes looked over the charcoal colored suit, the purple silk tie that shone beautifully beneath the light of the room. The jacket of his suit fit perfectly over his broad shoulders, and his pants hung seductively off his waist. He truly was a beautiful man, but inside him was nothing more than poison, death, hatred and rage.

"We should hurry, I want to get this picture out of the way, so we won't be late to the ballroom." Reaching for her hand, he grasped her fingers between his, squeezing them before leading her out of the bedroom and down the corridor to the living room. Her eyes glanced at the men dispersed throughout the room, not being given much time to look at each one when Joseph dragged her quickly through the room.

Entering the office that hadn't been used by Joseph since they moved in, Arianna saw a man standing to the side, camera equipment set up in order to capture their image.

The photographer pointed to an area he had set up before they'd arrived. "Joseph, if you would take a seat in the chair and Arianna, you should stand behind him. I'll make this quick so that you can move on to more exciting events for the evening."

Joseph chuckled at the photographer's words, and then took a seat where the photographer had asked. Taking her place, she blinked against the bright lights that beamed down on them. A few flashes of a fake smile, and the picture was done. She hated it. They hung in the halls of her wing, a reminder of the false perfection of her life. Every year he had one made, except for when it came to Aaron. Ever since the child had been born, Joseph insisted on monthly photographs, his pride in his son evident in the way he bragged. She heard him describe Aaron as his greatest accomplishment, a thing that would make him immortal, would help him cheat even death.

Having finished the sitting, Arianna followed behind Joseph out of the suite and down the long corridor to the ballroom. The two guards moved instantly to open the doors, welcoming Joseph to a throne room of sorts. A hush fell over the waiting audience, dark souls that reveled in the lifestyle that Joseph had created for them. Climbing the stairs, Arianna allowed a numbness to fall over her mind and her body. It was the only way she could witness the horrors that

Joseph would command – it was the only thing keeping her sane after taking part in the execution of the men who dared cross her husband.

After taking their seats, Joseph called the meeting to order and requested Emory to escort the accused inside from wherever it was they were kept. Arianna looked over to the doors of the west wing, not surprised when they walked a man in, but suddenly becoming horrified to see that a woman carrying a baby, and a small boy were walked in behind him.

She bit her tongue to keep from crying out, her eyes tracking the family as they were being led to the center of the ballroom. The mother was crying, her short brunette hair hanging lifelessly around her face while she looked at the child in her arms. The silence in the room was agonizing; she didn't know what to think or what her husband had planned to do to the people standing before them.

"Gregory Shipp. You've been caught stealing money from my network, from all of the men in this room, from my wife who sits beside me."

Arianna fidgeted in her chair, not appreciating that he'd attached her in any way to what he was about to do.

Standing, Joseph walked towards the front of the stage, the click of his heel a death march as he approached the scared man. "You've been a member of my network for quite some time, Mr.

Shipp, and as I'm sure you are aware, there have been three other occasions where some ignorant fool has attempted the same thing." Joseph paused before pacing the front of the stage and asking, "Do you recall what happened to those men?"

The scared man looked up, his mouse brown hair falling back, revealing areas where his hair was thinned and balding. "Yes, Joseph. The men were executed, they were shot."

Joseph nodded and folded his hands behind his back. Stopping before the man, he remained quiet for a moment, a faint cough sounding from one of the men sitting at the tables throughout the room.

"They were. So I assumed, as someone who's seen that, you would have known better than to attempt the same thing. However, since I am obviously wrong for having assumed that, I realize that I need to step up the punishment. Shooting a man isn't enough, is it? You still thought you could steal from The Estate. So, Mr. Shipp, I'll be stepping up the punishment tonight, hopefully deterring the next ambitious soul who thinks he can cheat the network."

The creak of the hinges of the doors to the right wing interrupted Joseph, and he turned, annoyed with the intrusion. One of his nameless men walked in and quickly climbed the stairs of the stage to whisper to Joseph. Her husband stilled, a bored expression on his face when he motioned for her to follow the man out of the room. She gladly complied, crossing the stage, only to feel Joseph's hand grip her arm before she could descend the stairs.

Leaning down to whisper in her ear, he instructed, "Deal with our son and return immediately to the ballroom when you are done." He released her and returned to his position on the stage.

Arianna climbed down quickly, letting her eyes glance at the small boy with wild brown hair and wide blue eyes that glittered from the light in the room. He appeared to be the same age as Aaron and the thought shocked her system more than she'd liked. He looked terrified and her heart broke for the young soul and whatever fate he would face.

She traveled through the corridor as fast as she could. The guard told her they were unable to silence Aaron, and that he'd woken from a nightmare and was tearing apart his room crying out for his mother. For as sweet as he was, Aaron had a vicious temper and she noticed that on some days she was only able to lull him back to sleep or help him keep calm by playing the song she'd written for him and had played for him since he'd been born.

Finally reaching her young son's room, she found him laid across his mattress, screaming into the blankets, his little arms and legs pumping furiously while he cried.

Sitting down beside him, she pulled his small body up from the mattress to cradle him against her. He calmed almost immediately, his small arms reaching up around her neck as he settled his head against her chest. She cooed to him, swaying him back and forth in an attempt to chase away whatever nightmare had scared him. Finally, when he had settled and his breathing grew deep and regular from sleep, she laid him back down on the bed, covering him with blankets before smoothing her hand over his head and kissing him on the cheek.

As soon as she stepped foot out of his room, the guard who had led her back from the ballroom returned her to the meeting, her shoulders were weighted with dread when they walked back, not knowing what she would find when they entered the large room. The creak of the large double doors announced her entrance and she almost fell to the ground when her eyes caught sight of what had transpired in her absence.

The father of the young family lay on the ground in a pool of his blood, his body positioned in a way that wasn't natural or possible without having bones broken and ripped out of joint. The screams of his wife hurt Arianna's ears as she watched the woman being dragged to a wooden table, crudely fashioned with four iron shackles drilled into the table. Arianna's eyes immediately sought out the two young children and an odd sense of relief blossomed in her chest when she saw the young boy sitting on the ground holding his sister in his arms. When

213

Arianna noticed what they intended to do with the mother, her breath caught and she raced to the boy's side and looked up to the stage to find Joseph standing above at the center front, a bored expression on his face while watching the men strip the woman of her clothes before fastening her to the table, each intimate part of her exposed to the crowd of men. Slowly, Joseph's head swiveled and when the molten grey of his eyes met hers, he yelled, "Stop!"

The men obeyed and stepped away from the table that now had a crying woman strapped to the rough wood surface.

"Arianna, so good of you to rejoin us. I need you to do me a favor." Gesturing down to the boy, he continued. "Xander here is going to be staying with us for a while, I thought he could be a good friend to our son considering they are around the same age."

The young mother began to wail, her small form obviously shaking from the emotions ravaging her body; fear, desolation, despair – it was a venomous cocktail that Arianna knew well.

Joseph rolled his eyes. Turning to his men, he asked, "Can someone please shut that woman up? I can't think with her screaming and crying like that."

The men complied immediately by placing a gag around her mouth and securing it at the back of her head.

Smiling once that had been accomplished, Joseph turned back to his wife. "As I was saying, please take the child back to your suite. He'll be staying with us indefinitely."

Arianna's head swam with disbelief, but she knew better than to argue with her husband. Kneeling down beside the child, his big blue eyes burned into hers. Red rimmed the skin of his eyes where he'd been crying and streaks of tears were clearly visible on his cheeks. She reached over, wondering why Joseph only referenced the boy when, clearly, there were two children. "May I take your sister from you, Xander, I promise I won't hurt her."

He nodded yes, his body quaking with fear as he reached up to hand her the small baby bundled in a blanket. Arianna breathed out as she accepted the baby, pulling the child to her chest and noticing that the child did not move or squirm in her hold. When she pulled the blanket back from the baby's face, she was met with a pair of lifeless eyes. Her heart fractured and her stomach threatened to expel its contents. Placing the baby down on the floor, she turned to the live child, saw the pain in his stare, and quickly took his hand to lead him from the room. "Xander, your sister is going to be okay, my husband just wants you to meet our son, Aaron. You'll like him, I can tell already that you two will have a lot in common, don't be scared, okay?"

He nodded, his fear paralyzing him to a point where he wouldn't speak. His tiny hand in hers, Arianna led him quickly from the room, shutting the doors behind them only to hear the echoed screams of his mother while the men continued whatever torture Joseph had ordered against the woman. Xander's body tensed and he tried to turn back for the doors. Arianna quickly picked him up and held him to her body, running down the hallways to escape the nightmare taking place on the other side of the doors that led into the mouth of Hell itself.

Chapter Twenty-Two

Her eyes burned with the threat of tears. Sitting on the floor by the toilet in her bathroom, Arianna sat back against the cool tile, incredulity filling her thoughts at the cruel irony that played constantly with her life. She could hear her stomach churn in the quiet room and she looked at the time on the clock that hung on the bathroom wall. She would have to get up soon, would have to force her body to move despite the sickness that crippled her so that she could tend to Aaron and Xander.

She'd suspected her condition for the past week, each day waking and looking to the calendar that hung on her bedroom wall. She was tired, she'd been drained of every bit of hope over the years she lived in the mansion, and now, she was late. Her ever-present tears resurfaced when she realized that she was pregnant once again, but this time there was only one man who could have fathered the child, and that man was the most depraved and vile bastard that existed.

Each day was a routine she kept with the children, the only sense of normalcy that could be found within a waking nightmare. She had no other companions besides the two children who every day stole her heart and gave her a reason to continue forward despite the hopelessness of her life.

Three more years had passed and the boys were now six years old. Over time, Arianna had watched as Aaron's eyes turned from a light blue, the same shade as hers, to an emerald green that was a startling reminder of a man Arianna had been forced to kill when Aaron was a baby. It broke her heart to look into his eyes every morning and be reminded of a gentle soul, one who'd been victim to the same violent lifestyle that haunted her daily life, and one who'd lost his life attempting to free her of her fate - to take her from the darkness into the possibility of light.

Joseph had to have noticed. When Aaron's eyes finally took on the jade hue, Joseph began to treat him differently, became more violent towards Arianna as a result. She was in constant fear for her life and the child's. She knew that Joseph's jealousy and rage could explode at any minute because of the clear and absolute reminder that Arianna had allowed another man to touch her in ways only Joseph had been allowed.

Day after day, Arianna worked through her daily routine with the boys, teaching them to read, to play music, allowing them outside so they could run and play like normal children. Her freedom to roam the grounds had been given back to her through the years, and on days where it was warm and the boys had energy to expend, she would walk them down to the stream. It broke her heart every time to see them playing on the rocks, and bravely exploring the cave where they pretended a dragon lived. With sticks held in their hands like swords, they would venture into the depth of that cave, fighting an unseen force while Arianna sat on the outside, drowning in the painful memories of Connor.

Aaron concerned her. Unlike Xander, who behaved like a normal child for the most part, Aaron had a violent streak to him, one that she attempted to temper through music. Even at the age of six, when he was prone to fits of rage, she would drag him, sometimes kicking and screaming into the music room and sit him down on the bench. As soon as her fingers touched the keys, he would calm and by the time he was four, he would place his hands beside her in an effort to elicit the same music from the ivory that she daily played for him. The music she'd written for him never left the stand above the keys, and she tried in vain not to think about the man who had snuck that music out of the mansion to have it transcribed and bound into a book for the baby that arrived shortly after she'd written it.

Xander liked to play the piano as well, but he was content with sitting back and listening to Aaron and Arianna. The boys' bond was unlike anything she'd seen. Xander and Aaron both looked out for each other even in their young age. It made her smile. There were times when they bickered like children will do, but for the most part, they protected each other, one never allowing the other to be pushed around. When one cried, the other one stood silently nearby, attempting to provide comfort by their mere presence in the room. Arianna was pleased to see that they provided each other with a sense of normality even in a place that was anything but normal.

By the time they turned five, Joseph had insisted they attend the network meetings in the ballroom. He believed that they would be made stronger if they were exposed to the dealings of the network from a young age. The first meeting left the boys shocked silent. Xander especially hated to attend, his young mind remembering what he'd seen done to his parents, to his sister, the first time he'd entered that room. It broke her heart to see them scared, utterly defenseless in a room of madmen. But when Aaron started to take on a bored expression, when he'd studiously watched the executions and the violence, and when it appeared he anticipated the death of the men condemned by Joseph, Arianna's heart broke. She would take the boys back to the rooms following the meeting, would sing Aaron to sleep while cradling Xander. It was the only bit of light she could provide to the boys – a mother's love.

And Joseph. She wouldn't have believed it possible for such a bright man to fall so far into madness as he had. His punishments became ridiculously cruel as the years went along. He reveled in the pain he caused, the looks of shock and satisfaction on the faces of his men. She never knew what he would do next and the constant fear of the unknown weighed heavily on her, aging her faster than normal.

Pushing herself up from the floor, she got dressed before walking to the boys' room to prepare them for their day. Like any day, they were difficult to wake, but once up, their energy levels exploded and they ran around the suite playing out games of cops and robbers, or pretended to be knights fighting against some unknown evil. After forcing them to sit and eat, she took their hands and led them to the music room. She allowed Xander to play first, but his interest in the instrument wasn't as deep-seated as Aaron's and after twenty minutes he'd had enough and chose to play with the scattered toys in the room while Aaron crawled up onto the bench and took a seat by his mother. Although his hands were still small, Aaron obviously carried her talent, having quickly learned the music and mastered an instrument as much as a young boy could. It was normal, it was good, and it was something that Joseph had started to despise.

. . .

"His features change daily, more and more I see the face of Connor. And his eyes, Joseph, have you not noticed how they've changed." Emory spoke quietly, hesitant in his agreement with something Joseph had suspected for the past year and a half.

Molten grey peered down at a recent photograph of the child he called his son. A small smile shown back at him; one that curled the ends of the child's mouth underneath a head of black hair and eyes the color of emerald. Dropping the photograph to the desk, Joseph sat back in his chair, folding his hands over each other. Every time he looked at the boy, the pride he'd had for the child dissipated and dissolved into a bitter resentment. His greatest achievement, the person that would make him immortal was not his. He knew it in his heart, in his very bones. Connor's ghost haunted him, a man that had intended to steal his wife, who had succeeded while pretending to be a loyal man that Joseph could trust. It sickened him, angered him and fueled the insanity that threatened to consume him.

"She embarrasses you, Joseph. How many more of your men does she fuck while you're not watching? How many of your personal guard walk the halls of your mansion, laughing to know that your wife is an unfaithful whore? She uses you and she no longer benefits you as she had before."

Emory's words rubbed against Joseph's nerves, grating in their truth. Arianna was like a living ghost, an empty shell of the woman she'd been when they'd first married. Contemptuous and cold, she laid like a limp rag beneath him when he visited her at night, stood silent by his side, never appreciating the life he created for her. Picking up the photograph once again, he crumpled the image between his fingers, tossing it aside from the rage that was building in his mind.

"Where is Arianna now?" Joseph's voice was quiet, but a dark edge hung to his words when they were spoken.

Emory smiled.

"She's teaching the boys music, wasting their talents on something that won't make them strong, that will only make them weak, unable to manage in a world as powerful as the one you've created. They'll embarrass you eventually."

"They embarrass me now!"

Emory sat back in his chair imitating Joseph's posture. A look of contentment spread across his face that finally, Joseph was listening to what he had to say. "Then kill them, Arianna...and the boys. Start over with one of the other women within the network.

Joseph remained silent, thoughtful. He couldn't kill the boys, couldn't risk doing something that would be undisputable proof of his failed marriage, of the unfaithful nature of his wife. "No. If I do that, it will be a weakness that the men could use against me." Sitting up, he opened a desk drawer containing the drug to which he'd become accustomed over the years. Scooping out a small dose, he prepared the drug before injecting it into his body; just enough to sooth the violent thoughts that battered at his mind.

Emory watched Joseph's face, waited for the drug to take affect, making Joseph's mind more malleable and ready for suggestion. When he saw the familiar haze creep into the steel grey gaze, he said, "It can be done quietly, so that nobody but those closest to you know the truth. Even then, I can lie; make up some reason why she no longer serves her purpose. The boys are at an age where she's not needed, they are at an age where they can become weak like the parents that made them, or strong – like you."

Smiling, Joseph sat back once more. Memories of a man who'd betrayed him flickering through his mind. "I kept Xander as a punishment to his parents. I could see the hatred they had for me in their expressions, the contempt towards a network that had fed them over many years." He chuckled. "The look on his father's face when I told him that his son would be raised by me, molded into the perfect soldier..."

"It was brilliant, Joseph. They'll never rest knowing their son will become like the man they abhorred." Emory finished the thought for Joseph, continued suggesting pure evil to a mind that was so obviously cracking. "And as for your wife, she's given you nothing that she promised, but rather she's handed you bitter lies and a child to raise that is not your own."

"And what do you think would be a fitting punishment?"

Emory's eyes glistened with anticipation. "I'm sure I could figure something out."

The two men sat silently as Joseph considered Emory's words. A decision finally settling in his thoughts he instructed, "Bring Arianna to me. I need to have to have a conversation with my wife."

Chapter Twenty-Three

"That's perfect, Aaron. Very good!" Arianna hugged her son to her side after he played the song she'd taught him perfectly. Pride shown in his green eyes, accomplishment of a task he'd been attempting for over a year. In truth, it wasn't his lack of intelligence or talent that had taken so long for him to learn – it was that his developing fingers hadn't been long enough to play, at least until now that he'd grown enough to master the keys.

Laughter and the sound of two small hands clapping sounded behind them and they turned to see Xander sitting on the couch in the room, covered completely in toys, his small face delighted to not have to share at that moment. Picking her son up from the bench, she placed him on the floor, her back protesting against the added weight of the boy who'd grown rapidly in size. They walked hand in hand towards where Xander sat, Aaron immediately grabbing some of the toys when he approached his friend. A small grimace broke out across Xander's face and Arianna laughed at his expression.

When the click of the door handle echoed across the walls, and when the hinges on the door creaked as it was pushed open, Arianna turned to look at the face of Emory, her eyes immediately traveling to the large, angry scar that ran from his ear to his chin; a reminder left behind by Connor on the night he'd attempted to help Arianna escape.

A sick smile spread across Emory's face as his eyes slowly traveled between Arianna and the boys. Bringing his demented gaze back to her, he said, "Joseph would like to see you."

Her eyes widened in surprise at the request. Joseph never asked to see her during the day and rarely did he still visit her at night. Dread crawled along her spine, but she plastered on a fake smile when she turned back to the boys. "I'll only be gone a moment, I'm sure your father just wants to check in and see how well the two of you are doing.

Aaron's eyes darkened, a blank expression painted across his small face when he walked to his mother and hugged around her waist, his little arms squeezing her tightly before letting her go. She leaned down and kissed him on the forehead and turned to Xander to kiss him as well. Xander laughed, he was such a happy child regardless of the circumstances of his life.

Turning to Emory, Arianna nodded her head and walked out of the room, replaced by two guards to watch over the children. Their footsteps sounded rhythmically as they traveled the halls, the large doors creaking when they entered the ballroom. The room was empty and Arianna turned to Emory with a confused expression on her face. "He waits for you in his suite on the west side." Her eyes widened impossibly more; Joseph had never allowed her into that wing since the year after they'd moved in. Her steps faltered, but Emory roughly grabbed her arm, dragging her to the doors on the opposite side of the ballroom.

When they entered the wing, her stomach roiled, fear and the remnants of morning sickness causing her insides to cramp painfully. The halls that were perfect mirrors of those in the right wing were deserted, and Arianna wondered how a group as large as the one she knew lived on this side could be completely absent.

Being led through the dead silence of the house bred more dread in her small body, her path more like a death march than a quick trip to visit Joseph.

Entering Joseph's suite, she looked around at the alcohol bottles and half empty glasses that filled the counters, tables and shelves. She winced at how a once beautiful room that she'd decorated with loving hands had been turned into what looked more like a bachelor pad than the family home she'd envisioned. Much like the halls, Joseph's suite was a mirror of her suite in the right wing. It was unnerving to step into a space so similar, yet so opposite to hers at the same time.

"He's in his office."

She didn't look back at Emory when he spoke. She hated him more than Joseph, knew that whereas Joseph had fallen into the state of insanity, Emory had been born like that; not a single cell within his body carried goodness or purity. Squaring her shoulders, she tilted her chin up, knowing that whatever she walked into would be bad.

. . .

Joseph looked up to meet eyes with the wife who he knew had never really loved him. He questioned her motives for having married him; a woman who came from meager beginnings to find herself attached to a man who had it all. He didn't want to believe it at first, didn't want to acknowledge that she used him for the life he provided her. And now, with the photograph of a child that looked more like a man he'd known than himself, he had proof that there was never love in the heart of his wife for him. Anger slithered along his mind, his nerves reacting, heat saturating his skin from the rush of blood.

"Sit down, Arianna."

She sat down, her crystal blue eyes opened wide while the skin on her brow furrowed in confusion and fear. Yes. Let her sit there quivering. If she wouldn't love him, she would at least submit to him – she would know that her value only lies in the husband to whom she was attached. He laughed to himself, the sad truth that he'd been stupid all those years a screaming realization within his thoughts. He'd provided everything for her, had rescued her from a life where she had no one except for a cousin who'd introduced her to the better members of society – to a life she didn't deserve. And now that the green eyes of truth shown back at him from the set of photographs that sat on his desk, Joseph accepted that she'd failed in her only duty, the only thing he'd asked of her in return.

It was a creeping embarrassment on the edges of his thoughts, the idea that through the years he'd never fathered a child with the woman who sat across from him. He thought he had, had pride in the son that he'd created. But she lied. His pride was shredded, his ego injured by the realization that he hadn't fathered a son, that he was somehow less of a man than a lowly guard.

It ate at him. Every time he saw her face, saw the flat expanse of her stomach despite the thousands of times he'd attempted to get her pregnant. It was a painful reminder, one he wanted eradicated from his life, from his home. He imagined her laughing at him, her knowledge of his failure a subject that brought amusement and joy. His eyes took in every detail of her face and body. The years had caused lines to cross her forehead; worried markings also surrounded her eyes and mouth. Her once shimmering hair hung limply by her face, and her skin hung off her body, the once toned muscle, lost over the years. It was a shame. She'd let herself go; and it was another mark against her.

He settled into his chair thinking Emory had been correct in his assessment. She had no purpose accept as a leach that fed off his efforts and his achievements.

Emory stepped into the room, walking towards the desk, stopping once he stood at Arianna's back.

With an expression that spoke of malice, Joseph said, "I was looking at a picture of *our* son this morning. It's his most recent – I'm sure you've seen it."

Arianna was silent but he saw her shoulders tense, her jaw suddenly clench at his words. It was all the proof he needed that she was aware of what he was about to say. Body language, it was the most honest thing about a person, it was the small hints that trickled from their brain to the outside. If a person knew what to look for, they would know they truth to what a man said, or the sincerity of the words they spoke. Her body language spoke of betrayal, of guilt – of fear. The fury that rolled through him was painful, his muscles clenching through his torso, his shoulders and his arms. He wanted her dead, he wanted to see the life drain from her eyes.

"Every time I look at my son, I'm reminded that the woman who was supposed to be my wife fucked another man. Not only did you dishonor me by fucking him, you had his child and allowed me to raise it as my own. You've managed to destroy me, Arianna; slowly, methodically, you've embarrassed me to my network and you've made me look like a fool for believing your lies."

He stood up from his chair, walked around the desk and sat against the wood surface so that he was directly in front of her. "I wanted one thing, one FUCKING thing from you for everything I've given you. And what do you give me?! Some fake bastard son?

"Joseph..."Arianna's voice trembled as she tried to interrupt.

"No! I do not want to hear anything you have to say. Everything that comes from that mouth of yours is a lie, a filthy fucking untruth that you use to continue taking from me." He laughed, his rage clouding logical thought. The taste of violence covered his tongue, his desire to punish, to ridicule and condemn. Her was drunk on power, but he still craved more.

With a bored expression, he leaned back on his desk. "You've outgrown your use, Arianna. You've become nothing more than a walking reminder of how I was betrayed in my own home, that I was deceived by the one person who should have loved me the most."

"Joseph please listen to me." Arianna pleaded with him, moved forward to place her hands on his knees and he backhanded her in response. She fell against the chair, blood splashing out at the corner of her mouth. Her bottom lip swelled where he had struck her and a small bit of satisfaction snaked its way through his veins.

Speaking over her sobs, he continued. "I have to keep Aaron, you know. You trapped me into raising the boy, hoping to God nobody notices that he's not mine."

"Joseph..."

He struck her again. "Stop fucking talking!" She cried harder and he groaned in disgust. "You have no right to cry you stupid bitch! You caused this! So yes, Arianna. I'll keep your bastard son; and despite his fucking crap genetics, I'll raise him to be like me...JUST like me."

She looked up at him suddenly, terror written across her face letting him know that he'd struck a nerve with that comment.

"Oh? You don't like that, do you? Can't handle knowing that your precious little boy will be raised by a man you so obviously despise." Another wicked chuckle, this one low in tone, rumbling deep in his chest. He smiled down at her, triumph written across his expression.

Arianna stilled. "What are you doing, Joseph?" Her eyes looked up at him, one swelling at the side from where she'd been hit. "Please, I have to tell you something..."

Lunging forward he grabbed her by the arms and lifted her from the chair with such force that the chair fell to the side, hitting the ground with a thick crack against the stone.

Forcing her up against Emory's chest, Joseph wrapped his hands around her throat, squeezed so tightly that her face instantly turned red and he could see the blood vessels break across her skin. In desperation to breath, her hands clawed at his, but he was too far buried within his rage to care that her fingernails tore at his skin. His eyes locked to hers and a smile peeked out from beneath the bored expression. Her eyes started to go out of focus, the lack of oxygen sending her deep into an oblivious tunnel. But he wouldn't kill her. No. That would be far too easy.

When she finally went limp in his hands, Emory's arms came up under hers to support her weight. Joseph released her neck, stood back admiring the marks left by the grip of his fingers. His eyes lifting to Emory's, he said, "She's all yours."

Joseph chuckled. "I'm sure she won't mind whatever you wish to do with her. She has a thing for guards."

A smile slid across Emory's face and he dragged Arianna's body from the room, disappearing down a long corridor while Joseph stood by his desk and watched her be delivered to her fate. He was empowered again, rediscovered pride settling within his body and mind for finally having conquered the one thing in his life that had betrayed him the most.

Chapter Twenty-Four

Arianna woke up slowly. Her arms burned where they felt like they were being pulled from her shoulders and her wrists felt like the skin had been ripped from the bone. Her head swiveled on her neck, and the room blinked in and out of focus while she struggled to wake up.

The tops of her feet brushed across the floor, but she placed them both down firmly, pushing up on her weak legs to decrease the pressure to her arms. The metal of the chains above her rattled with her movement and when she was finally able to fully open her eyes the room came into view.

With a quick glance it looked like the spare bedroom she'd decorated; but closer inspection revealed the filth on the floors, dried blood ground into the grout between the stone tiles. A fetid smell permeated the walls and air and the bed stood in the center, disheveled with stained blankets. She fought not to get sick, her already sensitive stomach contesting the putrid scent.

She was alone in the room and she quickly surmised that she was chained to a wall, left hanging by whoever had placed her there and left alone to wake up. She remembered Joseph choking her, and that his guard, Emory, held her while she lost consciousness. The chilled air against her skin told her that someone had removed her clothes and she trembled at the thought of what was to be done to her.

Arianna didn't know who'd be walking through the door of the room. She couldn't believe it, but she actually prayed it would be Joseph. She couldn't stand the thought that Emory would be allowed to touch her. Her prayers weren't realized, however, and within the hour, Emory entered from the hall.

"Oh, good. You've woken up. We can get this started finally." Emory's voice had the tone of a man diseased.

Arianna's body grew cold, sweat breaking out on her skin from fear of being left alone with Joseph's guard. "What are you doing? Where's Joseph?"

Emory snickered, his laugh as disgusting as his voice. "He doesn't want you anymore, told me I get to play with you now. Aren't you excited?"

Approaching her, one hand came up to rub along her stomach and breasts, while the other moved between her legs. Her body retched and she attempted to move away from him despite the chains that bound her to the wall.

"Oh, yes. This will be so sweet. I've been wanting to fuck you for years, Arianna." He chuckled. "I just didn't want to take the chance of ending up like your boyfriend. I knew Joseph would eventually grow tired of you."

"Emory, you need to stop. I'm pregnant...it's Joseph's child. You have to go get him so that I can tell him." Arianna begged with everything she had. She hated lowering herself to the sick man that stood before her, but she had not choice if she was going to save her life.

Sadly, Arianna didn't care if she lived or died, but when she remembered the two boys she'd left in the music room, she knew she had to fight – for them. Her heart felt like it broke into slivers at the thought that Aaron and Xander would have no one if something were to happen to her. She couldn't stand it, the thought of never hugging them again, playing music with them or watching them play.

"Oh, God, Emory, PLEASE go get Joseph...he needs to know!" Her voice creaked out around the pain Emory's touch was inflicting on her body. She begged and screamed for him to stop, but his hands, his mouth and his teeth explored every inch of her skin, forced sensations through her that made her want to die where she stood. "Please...."

Emory laughed, the heat of his breath moving over her skin before he stood up to look her in the eye. Reaching for his belt, Emory licked his lips. "I won't be telling Joseph anything except for how good it felt to fuck you as you died. Trust me, baby, after a few hours, you won't be pregnant any longer. I intend to enjoy myself tonight."

Arianna fought against the chains while screaming out for her husband. She was desperate for him to hear her, to come in the room so she could tell him why he couldn't let Emory do this. But it was no use. After a few minutes, her throat became raw and she could barely squeak out a sound. Emory stood watching her silently, his eyes turning an impossible black he reached for his pants and unbuckled them to let them fall to the floor.

"You're screwed, Arianna." A evil laugh rumbled through his chest. "Literally."

Grabbing her hips with his hands, he turned her so that her face was pressed against the wall. He lifted her towards him, shoving inside her so forcefully, that her nose bled from where it impacted with the wall. It didn't take long for him to finish and start again, ripping apart the sensitive flesh of her core and her ass. She could feel blood trailing down her legs within minutes and she screamed for Joseph the entire time despite the pain in her throat.

When Emory had finished he stepped away from her. Taking his cock between his hands, he looked over the blood and laughed when he raised his red hand to show her the stain. "And to think...that's just the beginning."

Emory moved quickly across the room and opened a drawer of a dresser and started pulling out tools and instruments. Arianna's jaw dropped and her eyes widened when she saw the knives, pliers, razors, and medical instruments he pulled from the drawer. She couldn't help herself and she threw up, the vomit trailing over her body adding to the horrendous smell of the room.

Emory looked over and smiled to see that she'd gotten sick. Tsking he made his way back over to her and ran his finger through the mess, forcing it back between her lips. "You dropped something."

She spit out instantly and he pulled his finger away laughing. "If you are trying to sicken me so I won't touch you, you're going to have to do a lot better than that, bitch."

Her head fell against the wall, tears forcing themselves from her eyes and the flood of emotions through her body crippling her legs below her. Uselessly she swung on those chains, but she couldn't find the strength to push herself back up. Her thoughts drifted to the past; memories of Connor, of laughing by the stream, the sunlight heating their skin in a place where they could escape their lives. She thought of the boys, of their laughter, their cries. She imagined both of them as they grew; heartbroken to know that she would never see them become adults. Absolute loss consumed her, but even with the intensity of that pain, it was easily shadowed by the pain of knowing her babies would be left to the will and instruction of a madman, that their lives would be drowned in the black pit that existed within Joseph's Estate. She thought about the boys faces as she left the music room and she died inside knowing it was the last time they would see each other.

Life wasn't fair. The fairy tales and stories she'd been told as a child were nothing more than fantasy, a dream that could never become true. There was no prince that arrived on a white horse, no frog that turned into the perfect man when kissed by the princess. No. Her life was anything but fair, an illusion of a future that she would never know, a light that was extinguished by the man she married so many years before. And now, she hung on a wall, given to a madman, a soulless bastard who reveled in pain, in blood, in death. She hated that he was the last person she would see, would know. So she closed her eyes, tried to go to a place where she could escape the room where she was trapped. She thought of her family, her old friends, but mostly she tried to see what awaited her when she died, wondered if Connor's soul was washed clean of the murders he'd committed when he'd given up his life trying to save hers.

She heard Emory when he moved back to the dresser and she opened her eyes when he selected a small blade. She didn't want to see what was coming, she wanted to stay in the place of beauty and light she'd just imagined. But she couldn't look away. Sliding back to where he took a position in front of Arianna, he smiled and held up the blade. "Do you know what I'm going to do with this?" In a singsong voice, he added, "I bet you don't."

Another sick laugh and he dragged the tip of the blade along her inner thigh, before resting it over the opening to her body.

Looking deep into her eyes, he pressed his forehead to hers. His rotten breath trailed over his face and she closed her eyes trying to hide the fear that she felt. He laughed.

"Ready for me bitch? We're about to have a really fun time."

Epilogue

Joseph stood proud looking at the fire that consumed his wife's body. Over the years and many deaths in his house, he'd found it easier to burn the remains than bury them. He'd had a field cleared down to the sand and a space erected to hold the corpses while they were turned to dust.

His hands folded at his back, he looked upon a thing that should have brought him great satisfaction. But instead, his heart sank into an abyss as the last bit of humanity he'd had left him was ripped from his chest.

He had to admit the bitch had claws.

It was irritating against his thoughts, the fact that even in death, she'd bested him.

The evening that she'd been dragged away, he'd sat in his office, allowed a whore to suck him off while the bloodcurdling screams of his wife echoed through the halls. He didn't know what Emory was doing to her and he didn't care. He felt gratification in the sound, it was a pleasurable music – one that fed the violence his soul craved. By the time he'd bent the whore over his desk, he'd released himself three times. But it wasn't the whore that excited him; it was the screams.

The morning hours approached, and she'd grown silent. He wondered if Emory had finally ended her life. Curiosity got the better of him and he ventured down the corridor to the room where she'd been taken. Opening the doors, he found her chained to the wall, stripped bare, blood dripping from almost every orifice of her body. He'd seen Emory's work before and it never failed to impress him, just how demented his guard could be.

When he looked over Arianna's limp body, her arms stretched above her head and her legs hanging lifelessly on the floor, he felt nothing. No pain, no remorse, none of the emotions he'd assumed he'd feel through the years if she'd died. Breathing a sigh of relief, he stepped into the room.

He approached her slowly - couldn't stop looking over what she'd become. Reaching out he went to move the hair from her face, and when she coughed, when blood sputtered from her mouth to the floor, he jumped back, surprised to find that she was still alive.

"How was it, beautiful? Did he treat you as well as the other guard?"

Her one eye looked up at him, the white surrounding the blue made red with broken blood vessels. Her other eye was missing. She spit out more blood from her mouth, and struggled for air. He expected tears, expected her to beg for him to release her, but when she smiled around the multiple cuts in her lips, his eyes narrowed.

"You should have listened to me, Joseph." Her voice was barely a whisper. She'd been held in that position for too long and had been beaten so thoroughly, it was cutting off her ability to breath. But even still, while slowly suffocating, she somehow found the determination and strength to state her final insult, a statement meant to mock her husband.

"Aaron...I don't know who fathered him. You're correct about that. But I did give you what you wanted, you would have been a father if..." She coughed again, red dribble escaping across her lips to slide down her chin. She breathed heavily, a loud wheeze present and the recognizable sound of fluid bubbling in her lungs.

"I'm pregnant, Joseph.... your child." She laughed, the sound was disturbing coming from a person in her condition. "All this time, all these years; the one thing you've always wanted...destroyed by your insanity."

His spine straightened and his muscles tightened over his tendons and bones, when he accused, "You're lying..."

"I'm not. I've known for a week, I was going to tell you, tried to tell you before..." Forcing herself to look up at him, she weakly said, "Do you remember that day in your office, the one when you told me that some of the best things are the one we must wait for?" She choked on a laugh. "For how much time it's taken, this child would've been special like you said...*a gift given to you when you least expected it.* And you destroyed it before it was ever given life." Her head dropped and her face looked to the floor when she added, "So much intelligence...so little common sense." Another curt laugh before her drowning cough. Her head fell, her strength giving out as her body weakened to a point of death. A rattle sounded in her chest and he grabbed her face, forcing her to look at him.

"Tell me your lying, Arianna, tell me..."

But it was too late. Her one eye still open, Joseph could tell that the light had left her. His fingers searched for a pulse, and finding none he let her body fall back against the wall.

Now he stood watching her body turn to dust. He hadn't wanted to believe her, had attempted to convince himself that she'd lied. Warring emotions raced violently through his mind, the idea that he could - that he had finally succeeded in fathering a child and the nagging belief she'd left with him that he'd destroyed his own immortality.

His mind fought violently against him. It couldn't be true, he tried to force the thought from his head, but it refused to release him. He'd never know, never be given the chance. And the nagging doubt and denial of truth was the last push over the precipice from genius to madness, the last nail in the coffin for Joseph's sanity.

He heard Emory's footsteps come up behind him. Twisted satisfaction written across the face of his guard when he finally took a position at Joseph's side. They stood silently watching the flames dance into the night sky. Normally there would be many men standing around the pyre, but on this night, it was a secret release of the life he'd known before The Estate had started, a silent disposal of the last person who dared betray him.

"What will you do with the boys? Have you decided to dispose of them as well?"

Irritation brushed across Joseph's mind. But he made promises to the parents of those children, had taken from them the thing that had always been denied to him. "No. They'll remain here."

"What are our instructions when it comes to them?"

Joseph sighed loudly, annoyed to be disturbed so quickly after Arianna's death. "I want them educated, trained. I believe both of them have the potential to be assets to The Estate. Aaron is still my son, Emory. Never forget that."

"But, his father was..."

"I don't want to fucking hear about that again. As far as this network knows, as far as the child knows, I am his father. I can raise him to be like me, to take over this network when I die. His life will still be a reminder of mine and that is all that concerns me. Perhaps I'll get one of the whores pregnant. If that happens, then Aaron may meet with an unfortunate accident."

Joseph turned to his guard. "Do as I instruct, Emory, without question."

Emory nodded his head and turned to walk back to the building.

Left alone, Joseph returned his focus to the flames. His eyes followed the black smoke that billowed out and covered the light cast by the full moon above him. When the flames had finally extinguished, when there was nothing left of the woman who'd torn him apart from the inside out, he stepped away.

He turned, walked slowly to the mansion lit brightly against the night sky. Joseph had gained what he needed, but it was still a stain, a small spot of imperfection that he would work diligently to cover up. He was certain that one day, Aaron would be nothing more than a mirror image of the man that raised him. He'd be a charismatic man that would be able to command a room just by his presence, he'd make Joseph proud and still remind the men of the network that Joseph had achieved it all.

Approaching the building, Joseph placed his hand on the door handle of the west entrance and pushed forward into his kingdom – it was a place that every man feared, a force so strong that it was respected by the authorities and criminals alike. And it was his. He ruled it.

And after him would be his son; a testament to Joseph's greatness, to his power and absolute strength.

Joseph had outshone Hell by creating The Estate. A perfect network, an unstoppable force, and because Joseph ruled it, he'd never be taken, never be destroyed and he'd go down in history known as the man who had achieved everything, had destroyed many, and who should be feared above all else.

Joseph reached his suite, closed the door behind him and allowed his eyes to fall on the young woman bound at her hands and feet in wait of what he would do to her. Laughing to himself, he stalked towards her, his pants growing tight when he thought of the violence to come.

The End

Other Books in the Estate Series:

Madeleine Abducted

Printed in Great Britain
by Amazon

30872321R00146